Snowplow Polka

Snowplow Polka

Ambrose McGuine

ROMANESQUE PRESS

Snowplow Polka
Copyright © 2016 David Atkinson and Valerie Atkinson
Romanesque Press
West St. Paul, Minnesota

Aside from brief passages in a published review, no part of this book may be reproduced or transmitted in any form or by any means, electronic or mechanical, including all technologies known or later developed, without written permission from the publisher.

To request reprint permission, e-mail Romanesque Press at romanesquepress@gmail.com.

This is a work of fiction. Names, characters, businesses, places, events and incidents are either the product of the author's imagination or used in a fictitious manner. Any resemblance to actual persons, living or dead, or actual events is coincidental.

Scripture quotations are from the ESV® Bible (The Holy Bible, English Standard Version®), copyright © 2001 by Crossway, a publishing ministry of Good News Publishers. Used by permission. All rights reserved.

Cover and chapter illustrations by Kevin Cannon
Page design by Trio Bookworks

Print ISBN: 978-0-9909668-0-7
Ebook ISBN: 978-0-9909668-1-4

Library of Congress Control Number: 2015951034

Manufactured in the U.S.A.

a **Trio Bookworks** *collaboration* | triobookworks.com

To Freda
Still polka dancing at 94

Contents

1. "Don't Worry, Be Happy" — 1
2. Geezer Power — 19
3. Cowbell Café — 33
4. We're Plowin' Now! — 45
5. Blood of the Lamb — 65
6. Memory Care — 75
7. Cold Turkey — 93
8. Village on Ice — 107
9. Dust Off Your Lederhosen — 125
10. Snowplow Polka — 141
11. Night Patrol — 157
12. Rap Polka — 169
13. Smite the Robbers — 179
14. Raise Your Cane — 197

"Don't Worry, Be Happy"

The buck that once did bound through the endless reaches of Wisconsin's Superior National Forest was now merely a trophy head, frozen in time on a knotty pine wall. His ferocious brother bear, the lumbering king of northwoods carnivores, was likewise reduced to nothing more than a rug. Its dense pelt was now splayed in submission before a stone hearth, a zigzag fringe of red felt giving it an aura of embarrassment. Only its head—with jaws parted in an eternal snarl and glass eyes glowering up at unseen conquerors—retained any dignity.

In the dimming blue winter light, many smaller creatures were gathered in a front room, as though for the wake of buck

Snowplow Polka

and bruin: the pheasant in flight, the fish in flop, a pine marten baring its tiny teeth—even the common gray squirrel, whose last expression of disbelief was somehow preserved during its stuffing. Unequal in size, they all shared the indignity of being reduced to props in a familiar diorama known as the lake cabin.

With summer's antics ended and autumn's hunting shack bravadoes also done, the cabin had been locked and left to hibernate when the half-year of winter began to settle in. The mummified congregation would have little to witness during this dreamless lull.

Still, if the offspring of the taxidermist's art expected any sympathy from the room's jumble of mismatched furniture, they would be sorely disappointed. An overstuffed sofa with a broken arm sat facing a lopsided recliner whose years of service had left its seat cushion a crackled map of good times long gone. The only other occupant of note was an outdated dinette whose boomerang-patterned Formica top and rippled chrome skirt were so out of style they were now shabby chic. The figures in this tableau were expected to remain undisturbed for months, until the lengthening spring days would at last breathe new life into their northern abode.

But suddenly the sound of shattering glass, followed by the creaking of a wooden window frame on its metal tracks made known an intrusion into this sealed place. A gust of outdoor air carried with it the impish giggles of teenagers on the loose.

Two dark figures bustled out of the back room and, after taking a few seconds to evaluate the threadbare choices in the confined space, grabbed a quilt from the sofa and tossed it on the floor. Then off came their parkas with a series of popping snaps and zipper rips. Crawling quickly onto the quilt, they hauled the matted bearskin rug over themselves while huffing in the frigid air.

"Don't Worry, Be Happy"

"Why do we have to break in to do this?" a girl whined peevishly. "The backseat of your car couldn't be any colder."

"A whiff of danger gets me juiced—it's like hunting," a boy answered huskily. "Under this bearskin you'll be sweatin' in no time."

"I don't see why we couldn't light just a little fire."

"Someone would notice that for sure. Old Mildred up the road can smell a squirrel fart across the lake."

"My shoes got full of snow climbing in that back window."

"We couldn't leave footprints to the front door, Mandy. That would be like telling the whole town we're here. If your clothes are wet, you better get 'em off quick."

"Very funny, Zach."

The dead bruin's pelt appeared to show some life again as the kids squirmed and laughed under it.

"Zach, shush! Did you hear something?"

"Yeah, that was my zipper goin' south."

"No, stupid! It sounded like tires or boots crunching."

Then, without saying a word, the two teens watched as shady forms crossed the front windows of the cabin, their shadows sliding over the furnishings. The front door knob squeaked as it was turned, but after a rattle of exasperation it stopped.

"Maybe it's Sheriff Trost," the girl whispered. "There's been a lot of cabin break-ins lately."

Outside, at least two male voices rumbled in gruff, inaudible dialogue. Hands cupped against the front windows shaded eyes searching for a vulnerable portal. When these attempts had failed, the mutterings ended with a loud curse and a bellowed command that put the teen lovers on red alert.

"You go check the back. If you can't get in there, I'll break the friggin' door open!"

Snowplow Polka

The prowlers outside switched on a flashlight with a beam so powerful the probing circle lit most of the front room.

"We gotta run for it!" the boy blurted.

"I'm naked as a jaybird, Zach!" Mandy yipped hoarsely.

"Keep the bearskin on! Run!"

Through the front window the intruders saw a shaggy, hulking form rise before their eyes. Exposed by their search beam, it was now erect and shaking, filling much of the meager living room.

"What the hell is that? We woke up some damn animal!"

"It looks like a friggin' bear. Get my gun out of the trunk."

The terrified kids raced toward the bedroom window they had pried open and practically leapt through it. The bitter cold air whipped exposed flesh as shoeless feet made hole after freezing hole in the icy snow. Not stopping when they arrived at the top of the steep hill that dropped off to the lakeshore, they slipped and slid awkwardly downward until they fell head over heels, descending like pinwheels of pale limbs and dark flapping bearskin into the slanting void.

Mandy witnessed the world pass by in quick stop-action images: dark branches against stars alternating with a white crystalline muff that smashed into her face with stinging slaps. Briefly, a third image entered the cycle: two figures silhouetted against the night sky at the top of the hill. Then she saw a flash from a rifle. After a deafening BAM, a blood-curdling scream of pain echoed over the frozen lake.

Rick Reinhart peered through the windshield of his Subaru Forester and watched the swirling snow spiral elegantly over

"Don't Worry, Be Happy"

the two-lane highway. His wife, Vicky, stared dreamily at the windblown scene from the passenger seat.

"When the snow makes those wispy funnels on the road it always reminds me of looking out from an airplane at blowing clouds," she said, breaking the spell of Rick's thoughts.

"Sometimes I think the sticky wet snow is easier to drive through," he replied. "When the wind whips this light fluff over the fields and right across the road, it's hard to tell where one ends and the other begins."

"We've made this trip so many times I feel like I could do it in my sleep." Vicky's voice was as soft as the dancing flakes.

I guess that's a nice feeling, Rick thought as the mostly colorless farm fields of white and brown rolled past their windows. Out of the corner of his eye he watched his wife twist a ringlet of her dark, naturally curly hair around her finger. Rick glanced instinctively in the mirror and swept a strand of thin blond hair off his forehead. The trip from the Twin Cities to his mother's rural lake home could sometimes feel arduous to him. Vicky had the right attitude, though. For her, the familiar turns, landmarks and snug villages were all part of a family routine, a ritual that bound them together.

From the backseat, the burbling whistles and beeps of children's electronic games added a cartoonish undercurrent to the road trip's soundtrack.

"Yes! It's a new unicorn for my stable!" Rick heard Tammy exclaim. "Just one more and I'll be able to buy a new pasture." The ecstatic eight year old turned her tablet toward her brother so he could see the latest addition. Scrunched into the other corner of the seat, Travis paused his own game and gave his sister a quick, insincere nod of approval. He was cocooned in chunky headphones and seemed completely

Snowplow Polka

absorbed in an electronic world of his own, which certainly involved no unicorns.

It's too bad the age difference keeps them from sharing more interests, thought Rick as he checked on the kids in his rearview mirror. Travis, with the same wavy dark hair and green eyes as his mother, was now twelve. The gap between a preteen and someone four years younger was pretty wide. One being a boy and the other a girl made the differences even more pronounced. *Thank God there are apps for that*, he conceded.

After a long drive, the last turnoff was on the horizon. Then, just as the Row Right Inn came into view, it was time for the customary family shout-out when a glimpse of Grandma's house could be seen across the lake.

"Alright kids, all together now," Vicky prompted, and the chorus of four called out, "One, two, three . . . There's Grandma's house!"

The growing anticipation, heightened by this rousing cheer, made the last two miles of country byways, past square plots of farmland, hard to tolerate. Nestled in a grove of oak and spruce trees, Mildred Reinhart's house was a large two-story cottage-style home with a tuck-under double garage, the last structure at the dead-end of a gravel road on the peninsula that jutted out into Little Butternut Lake. With its shingle and lap siding, painted barn red with white trim, it was the only year-round dwelling on the last stretch of 2¼ Street. All of the other buildings they passed on the way to the Reinhart driveway were much smaller seasonal cabins.

Although everyone referred to it as "Grandma's house," in truth it was now Grandma and Ollie's house. It had been seven

"Don't Worry, Be Happy"

years since Rick's dad, Virgil, had died and three years since his mother, now seventy-eight, had attracted the attentions of a retired bachelor farmer, Oliver Rolloff, now eighty. This suitor sprang from the retirement center and took up housekeeping with Grandma in the lake home Rick's folks had built together. Virgil had always wanted to live by the lake, and, after selling the family farm, had finally been able to afford this dream home. Ollie certainly wasn't a bad guy, Rick reminded himself, just a semi-loveable elderly gent with the inevitably ingrained habits of anyone who had wandered around planet Earth for eight decades. Still, it was hard to completely trust someone who had lost his farm to an investment scam and continuously concocted harebrained get-rich-quick ventures that never seemed to pan out.

The cabins along 2¼ were closed and boarded up for the winter. Grandma Millie always complained about these fair-weather neighbors, who saw such an idyllic spot as merely a summer diversion. Winter was so beautiful and peaceful—how could anyone fail to recognize its charms? Rick thought this isolated setting was one of many reasons it was good for his mom to have a companion like Ollie. She wouldn't be all alone out here, and she'd have someone to help her, someone to talk to, someone to enjoy fussing over.

When the Reinhart family rolled into Grandma's driveway, an unfamiliar vehicle loomed outside the garage.

"Is that one of your uncle's trucks?" Vicky asked.

"I've never seen it before," Rick replied.

Rick's car took on a toy-like appearance as it crunched to a halt next to the white behemoth. Someone had further exaggerated the size of the hulking F-250 SuperCab by jacking up the frame to accommodate oversized tires with chunky treads. An array of hazard lights was mounted to the roof, and the framework for supporting a plow blade was secured to the muscular front bumper. The unattached blade rested in front of the second garage stall.

As Rick got out of his Forester, he noted that the F-250's running boards were as high as his waist. *You'd need a step stool to get into that thing*, he mused.

The stillness of the frozen landscape was pierced by Mildred Reinhart's cheerful greeting. "For goodness sake, look who's here!"

Travis and Tammy piled out of the backseat of the compact SUV and hurried over to their grandmother. Tammy danced around until Millie trapped her in a tight embrace and said, "Come here my little blue-eyed bunny—stop your bouncing and give grandma a hug!"

Travis hung back until Millie latched onto his jacket and dragged him into the circle. "And what about you, handsome? Do you think you're too old for a smooch?"

Tammy giggled as her brother awkwardly accepted a loud kiss.

Another voyage safely completed, Rick thought, watching his kids' reactions happily. As Rick and Vicky took in this homey scene, they gradually became aware of a strange anomaly: while their whole family was decked out in vibrantly colored winter gear—dangling tassels, down parkas and clunky boots—Millie was receiving them in a faded floral housecoat and cotton ankle socks.

"Mom! Where's your jacket? Your boots?" asked a concerned Rick.

Millie waved him off as if the blowing snow was an inconvenience unworthy of attention. "I've got my socks on—that's always enough till it gets real cold out."

"But Grandma, it *is* cold out!" exclaimed Tammy.

"Don't Worry, Be Happy"

The kids nudged Millie ahead of them toward the front door of the house. Rick returned to the car to start unpacking, shaking his head in amusement.

After most of the luggage had been piled in the front entryway, before taking it to the second-floor bedrooms, Rick walked into the combined living and dining room with its knotty pine vaulted ceiling. Vicky and the kids had followed Millie and the scent of freshly baked cookies into the kitchen. Rick had expected to see other visitors as he scanned the main room, with its two-story fieldstone fireplace and long row of windows looking out to the lake. To his surprise, the only occupant of the room was Ollie, who was slouched on the worn sofa, surrounded by piles of paperwork. The elderly gentleman was scrutinizing the fine print in a booklet. He stopped, and peered over the top of his reading glasses.

"Rick, Rick, I'm glad you're here. You drive a Ford, don't you?" Ollie took off his glasses and ran a hand through his silver white hair while he waited for Rick to answer.

"Subaru," was the younger man's reply. "I did have a Gran Torino once. By the way, whose truck is that outside?"

Even as the words left his lips, a feeling of apprehension caused Rick to look again at what Ollie was reading—an owner's manual.

"That's mine," came the chipper retort. "Well, mine and your mother's. Isn't she a beaut'?"

Rick tried to stay composed. "You didn't trade in the Buick, did you?" His wool stocking cap and winter coat suddenly felt quite hot and uncomfortable.

"Oh heck no! I'd never get rid of that classic. Now, before

you take your jacket off, I want you to come out and look at something with me." Ollie rolled out of the paper nest that surrounded him and, with a stiff, left-leaning gait, veered toward the coat rack by the front door.

Once outside, Rick noticed that Ollie still had the owner's manual in his hand. They approached the imposing vehicle.

"Are we going to attach the plow blade?" asked Rick.

"I don't need to do that now. I got to check the oil and other fluids first, but I had trouble raising the hood. Sometimes the simplest things can be so confounding."

How could I find a more apt metaphor for why you shouldn't own this truck? Rick thought to himself.

"All it says is 'Release lever under dashboard, then depress hood latch.'"

"That sounds like standard procedure," affirmed Rick.

"Well, I released the inside handle, but I couldn't find any latch under the hood."

Rick approached the vehicle's menacing grill and slipped his gloved fingers under the slightly raised hood. Sure enough, he couldn't locate a latch where he expected it to be either. He tried the other side next, but again, nothing. Then he peered into the crack, but there wasn't enough light to see anything. "You usually feel the lever in the center," he stated.

"That's what I thought. How can opening the hood be so dang hard? And I even read the manual!" exclaimed Ollie.

Rick rolled his eyes. *When all else fails.*

A flashlight beam aimed from the side finally revealed a hook-shaped object right in the middle, partially hidden by the hood's chrome center strip. Ollie and Rick both worked to depress the rusty latch but it wouldn't budge. So Ollie grabbed a footstool for height and a long screwdriver for leverage. He commanded Rick to keep the flashlight steady and then clam-

"Don't Worry, Be Happy"

bered onto the F-250's bumper and threw his weight against the screwdriver's handle while the tip was wedged against the latch. With a creaking pop, the corroded fastener relented and the hood sprang up, launching Ollie into the air. Rick jerked his head out of the way of the metal sheet and quickly turned to see what had happened to the older man.

Ollie had landed in the stiff branches of a yew bush next to the driveway. He was thrashing around in the snowy shrubbery, trying to find support. Rick ran to help the flailing man and was amazed to hear him cackling with glee.

"Damn, what a trip! That baby really packs a wallop!" Ollie wheezed.

He seems downright pleased about it! Rick thought. *Maybe he's happy for the chance to prove he's still got it. I suppose he thinks he's "Built Ford Tough."*

"Fire up the Weber!" Vicky called out as the two men trudged back into the living room.

"So keep my jacket on?" Rick asked.

"Yep—do you want to eat tonight?" Vicky replied as Rick walked past the kitchen and along the hallway toward the door that led to the garage.

"I'm going out to get the charcoal," he called back. "Could you bring me some newspaper to get it started? And tell Travis to get that luggage upstairs."

Standing outside on an exposed patio while keeping coals alive in an outdoor grill with the winds of November blowing around him was always a bit tricky, but it would be nice to keep his mom out of the kitchen for once so she could spend time with the grandchildren.

Snowplow Polka

Still, Millie objected. "I've got a roast in the freezer that we can take out for dinner. It's the perfect size for company."

"You save that roast for another special occasion," Vicky said, trying to redirect her mother-in-law. "Rick and I brought a whole cooler of food today so you wouldn't have to cook for us. You just sit back and visit with Travis and Tammy."

Vicky walked over to the sofa and made eye contact with the kids. "You guys put those video games away and get out Grandma's Mexican Train board game. You know how she loves playing that with you."

Out on the frigid cement patio behind the garage, Rick stood near the Weber to monitor its glowing heart. He thought that its ageless design made it look for all the world like a descending spacecraft and wondered if they still produced it in this avocado shade. The raw wind found its way around the bottom of his parka, but Rick didn't want to leave the sirloin strip steaks unattended. It would be worth the effort to serve something everyone liked and to avoid the question of what undated mystery meat might otherwise emerge from his mother's freezer.

After shielding the grilling meat from the wind for one last check, he went in for a warm platter, rushed back out to flip the still-sizzling steaks onto it, and quickly headed back inside to the round oak dining room table.

"Now do I get to take off my coat, dear?" Rick teased.

"Yes, dear, and thank you." Vicky came over and gave him a kiss. "Wow, these steaks looks great! Gather round the table, everyone. Let's eat!"

"Nice work, Dad!" added Travis.

"Oh my, have you ever seen such a slab of meat?" This praise, from Millie, was also a preamble for a demonstration of competitive frugality and a lecture on the joys of under-

"Don't Worry, Be Happy"

indulgence. She opened the game by cutting the smallest steak roughly in half and leaving the larger portion on the platter. "This is way too much for me. Ollie and I never eat such large meals. This size steak, even if we bought steak, which we don't, would last us a week. I'll save the other half for supper tomorrow. Sometimes Ollie and I just split a can of peas at dinner—they're surprisingly satisfying." Millie blew a kiss at her beau, who winked back.

With this bet on the table, Ollie saw her hand and raised it. Cutting the remaining half steak into two smaller pieces, he took only one of them. "Dear me, I can't remember when I last made such a glutton of myself," he moaned.

Sensing a bluff, Millie returned her half steak to the platter and instead took half of the piece Ollie had left and said, "And it would be such a shame to waste so much meat in one day! We could have stroganoff tomorrow, and French dip sandwiches the day after that."

She gazed into Ollie's twinkling eyes and queried, "What is a half of a half of a half?"

"An eighth," Travis replied flatly.

When everyone had finished that to which they felt entitled, the family addressed the usual obligations of seeking updates on relatives and friends. Rick waited for the right opportunity to present his case regarding the question of whether the oversized truck his mom and Ollie had purchased was really necessary.

As luck would have it, while the leftovers were being sealed away in Tupperware containers, Vicky mentioned an interesting finding that Rick thought would open the door to a conversation about the safety of two senior citizens living alone in an isolated setting.

"When I was bringing Rick the newspapers, I happened to notice that the front page of the *Upper Mainz Rheinlander* had an article about a disturbing incident. It said there had been a cabin robbery right in your area."

"Robbery!" Travis and Tammy exclaimed. Tammy got up from the table, ran over to her grandma, and put her arms around her neck.

"Oh, for crying in the soup!" Millie sputtered as she shooed her granddaughter away. "One harmless incident and that busy-body Rupert Everson has to tell the whole world about it."

"He does write the newspaper," Rick countered with an eye cocked at his mom.

"You call that news? A couple of teenagers break into a closed cabin? In my day we would whip their behinds and make them fix the damaged window."

"It looked like a lot more than just teen pranksters from what I saw in the article," said Vicky. "A gunshot was fired, and a local boy was hurt."

"Zach Garber, yes," Ollie agreed. "Just grazed on the butt cheek, but yah, he was shot."

"Butt cheek!" Travis snorted. "You said 'butt cheek.'"

"And what about the other people? The ones who shot at them?" Vicky probed.

"Good heavens!" Millie griped. "That *Rheinlander* makes it sound like we're in some kinda war zone here." Her protestations continued, but she knew her arguments were running out of steam.

"Well, there was a robbery attempt right in your neighborhood. At least one gunshot was fired, and a boy was injured," Rick concluded. "You didn't think that was news?"

"Don't Worry, Be Happy"

Millie and Ollie looked at each other sheepishly. Maybe the incident was more serious than they had wanted to admit.

Rick was genuinely concerned about the elders, but he was also quite pleased that this revelation had shamed them some. With a stern demeanor, he built momentum for his important presentation: the case of the too-big truck.

"You know we love you, we worry about your safety, and we don't live nearby in case an emergency arises," Rick said sincerely. "So that leads me to the question I have about this purchase of yours. I'm disappointed that you two would buy such a giant truck without talking to us first." He paused, and, hearing no objection, decided to press on. "That vehicle seems like way more capacity than you need here. It just looks too large for you guys to handle."

Rick had been determined to make his opening argument a strong statement and leave no room for misinterpretation about how worried he was. Going with the word "disappointed" had been harsh but necessary, he felt. When his self-evident facts brought only blank stares, he sensed an easy win and forged ahead with the sustaining evidence for his case.

There was a brief silence after he finished, and then the defense came out swinging.

Millie spoke out first. "That truck was a great deal, and it's not a waste, it's an investment!"

"Your mom's right," Ollie confirmed. "We're going into the snowplowing business, and that baby is just what we need."

"Business . . . snowplowing business?" This possibility had not crossed Rick's mind.

"Yes, business!" Millie exclaimed. "We never criticize the stupid things you kids do! How feeble do you think we are? I just got my driver's license renewed, and it's good for five more years. Don't say I got no 'old timers' disease."

Snowplow Polka

"Alzheimer's," Rick corrected, but his head was now swimming from the realization that the truck was only the beginning of his worries.

"Who would hire you?" Rick's tongue was slipping while his brain worked to find traction. "That's cold, dark, dangerous work, and now there's robbers in the area, with guns! You're both eighty!"

Ollie had gone red, and he thumped a serving spoon on the table like a gavel. "Who would hire us? How about the Village of Upper Mainz?"

"They know good workers when they see them," Millie stated, perhaps imagining herself rebutting the false testimony of larcenous guardians while Judge Judy looked on approvingly at her moxie. "I'm only seventy-eight. They fired that no-good Swany Swanson because he was too darn old and Sheriff Trost found him drunk on the job."

Ollie continued where Millie had left off. He clearly had a litany of the former plow driver's misdeeds memorized. "Swany couldn't even get out of bed some mornings when Lucille phoned him. And he knocked our mailbox clean around with the plow wake. And ours wasn't the only mailbox he rammed all to hell—Nelsons and Thompsons said the same thing. And Joey Muska found a chunk of his lawn ripped out from the blade and a fence post split right in half."

This roster of witnesses included many a known bigwig in town: Lucille the village clerk, Helmuth Trost the sherrif, a parade of neighbors and farmers all crying out for justice.

"But Mom," Vicky implored, "we're just saying we're worried about you and Ollie. Right? Think about the dangers of snowplowing." Vicky meant well, but her arguments didn't sway the court. Before long she threw her hands into the air and began carrying dishes to the kitchen.

"Don't Worry, Be Happy"

The kids had long ago drifted away from the table and were back in the living room making domino trains with Grandma's game.

Nothing could have better illustrated the hobbled condition of Rick's arguments than the fact that Ollie and Millie were paying more attention to the Mexican Train's progress than to his closing statement. They both laughed as the game board emitted a squawking-chicken screech. "Sounds like somebody started a double!" Millie whooped.

"Lucille actually asked you to take on this work?" Rick heard the first weak notes of conciliation seep into his question.

Millie turned back to Rick and replied, "She thought we'd be great at it. We know every back road and driveway in the neighborhood. We don't have to do the major county roads or the highways—the township plows do that." The happy woman displayed the broad smile of a vindicated defendant.

"On Monday we sign the papers in town. Helmuth will be there, too." Ollie added. "The village will benefit by having two upstanding citizens on the job."

Rick thought his mom and Ollie might break into chest bumps and high fives as they gloated about the near-universal approval of their new business venture. But they satisfied themselves further with a series of venerable and time-worn clichés: "You should be glad we can still make money. We've been on a fixed income for years. The price of everything has just gone sky high. We haven't had a Social Security raise in two years. How much is gas in the Twin Cities?"

It was now obvious that Rick's deflated case would be thrown out for lack of evidence. He saw the discussion was over. No one paid much attention as he rose slowly from the table, crossed the living room and headed toward his dad's old home office. He opened the louvered doors and stepped into this retreat, which housed a collection of Reinhart memorabilia. In the center of the room sat an oak desk where family business had always been conducted. Along the side and back walls there were filing cabinets and bookcases. Rick passed the bookcase on his right on his way to admire a grouping of family photos, awards and mounted game fish on the far wall, only to jump back as one of the animals flipped its tail, stretched out from its wall plaque and began lip-synching to a recording of "Don't Worry, Be Happy."

"Isn't that the funniest thing?" Millie called out from the living room. "I meant to show that to you kids."

"That's 'Big Mouth Billy Bass,'" Ollie chortled. "When you walk close enough to him, he turns on and starts singing. He's got two different songs."

I guess that puts it in a nutshell, Rich thought as Tammy and Travis came running in and incited Big Mouth Billy Bass to repeat his two-song cycle continually while they convulsed with laughter.

As Rick left the office he stopped, leaned against the door frame and looked at his mother seated in the living room rearranging dominos on the coffee table. "So Swany Swanson actually got fired?" he asked.

"Yup, they sent him down to Florida to live by his daughter. Maybe she can get him to sober up." Millie said.

"How old is Swany, anyway?"

"Seventy-nine. I think."

Geezer Power

The light layer of packed snow and gravel in the White Pines parking lot made a squeaking crunch as Millie and Ollie got out of their Buick and walked toward the tavern's backdoor. The rear parking area alternated between darkness and pools of glaring illumination under floodlights attached to telephone poles. No one from town used the main entrance, even though it featured a welcoming front porch under a faded roof-mounted sign in the shape of a leaping walleyed pike wearing a top hat who looked enthusiastically toward County Road P. This facade existed only to lure uninitiated tourists into the tavern.

Snowplow Polka

"That's funny, I don't hear any music." Ollie sounded befuddled. "It's Sunday night, isn't it? Reggie always plays on Sunday night."

"Of course it's Sunday, Oliver." Millie replied in exasperation. "We just managed to get the kids out the door. They have to be back to work and to school in the Cities tomorrow, ya know."

Ollie looked around at the cars and trucks in the parking area. "There's people inside, that's for sure, the lot's almost full."

Carrying plastic bags containing their dancing shoes, they proceeded cautiously, watching for patches of ice. Ollie had the cuffs of his suit pants tucked into rubber barn boots, and Millie's nylon-clad feet were inside flat-bottom booties.

"It looks kinda dark in there, too." Millie said.

Sunday night's dance usually generated a rollicking hoopla of polka music at the roadhouse. They slowed to a stop and warily opened the storm door. Before they could reach the handle on the oak-planked inner door, it flew in as if hit by a gust of wind. A jovial crowd whooped and clapped as the lights cranked back up in the hallway that opened to the main room of the bar. Reggie the accordion player broke into a lively rendition of "For He's a Jolly Good Fellow." The rest of the Upper Mainz Polka Club assembled on the wooden dance floor in the center of the bar's main room. The revelers sang along to the anthem or blew a tooting accompaniment on empty beer bottles.

"What in God's name is all this fuss about?" Ollie gaped at the animated bar patrons, who crouched lower as they sang, "Which nobody can deny, which nobody can deny" before leaping back up to begin again with "For he's a jolly good fellow."

Geezer Power

Millie tried to focus on her sister-in-law Eunice, who was shouting happy proclamations close to her ear. "You did it! You two did it!"

"Did what?" Millie asked, honestly confused.

"Everything!" Eunice expounded. "Got your truck, started your business, and sent those doubting kids back to the Cities with a little attitude adjustment."

Millie wondered how the dancing group could already know about the plowing business or Rick and Vicky's arguments against their well-laid plans. Then a lightbulb went on in her head. Rick must have phoned his Uncle Richie and Aunt Eunice. That was it! Rick had gone upstairs to the guest bedroom for quite awhile. He must have been phoning everyone in the family behind their backs, trying to get someone to agree with him that she and Ollie had gone off their rockers with this snowplowing idea. Well, it looked like just the opposite had happened. Richie, her younger brother, must have told him that Ollie and Millie could make their own decisions, and now everyone in town knew about the argument in the family and who had won.

Another chorus of cheers rang out.

"Hail to the seniors!"

"Geezer power!"

"Your granny wears snowshoes!"

"Don't forget to plow out the senior center first, so breakfast is on time."

"Well I'll be a blue-nosed gopher!" Ollie exclaimed while slipping into newly polished cap-toed shoes. "I say, let's all have a dance!"

Snowplow Polka

Reggie adjusted the strap of his accordion and made sure his tambourine leggings were set for some jangling percussive accompaniment. The White Pines Tavern could only afford a one-man-band, but everyone agreed that Reggie VanArsdale was all anyone could ask for. He even attracted more dancers than just the county regulars. In Millie's opinion it was too bad he especially attracted so many single women. There was already a surplus of lonely ladies looking for partners around Upper Mainz. She'd had to watch Ollie like a hawk and put her foot down on a few cheeky broads who couldn't help but get fresh with her man. Just because they weren't officially married didn't mean there weren't any rules.

The musician buried the foam-balled microphone deep into his bushy mustache and brought the zany crowd back to order by whispering the lyrics of the next song, set to a slower schottische, rolling his eyes in a display of innocence and suggestiveness worthy of Benny Hill.

> Is there a lump in your trousers, dear Elmer,
>   dear Elmer? . . .

Couples began to slide out of the booths that lined the pine paneled walls, and others got up from tables scattered around the room. They crowded onto the polished maple dance floor, stepping lightly to each first line and then in unison shouting and clapping out the chorus, "That just depends, that just depends."

> Is there a lump in your trousers, dear Elmer, dear Elmer?
> That just depends, that just depends.
> Looks like you're thinking about me, dear Elmer.
> That just depends, that just depends.

Reggie then switched to a high falsetto and trilled the next section of his ditty with the floating sweetness of a schoolgirl.

> Oh you make me feel just like a little girl.
> May I take your hand now and show you how to twirl.
> When it comes to the dancing, there's no courage
> > in the boys.
> But all the kids say, "That Mabel's got poise."

After that, it was time to step and pause again to the "dear Elmer" chorus, before Reggie morphed back into the pining wee Mabel.

> I feel just like a Barbie who never found her Ken.
> All the boys played hide and seek, while I counted
> > up to ten.
> But when you said, "You're it, girl," I forgot my other
> > toys.
> Yah, all the kids say, "That Mabel's got poise."

Hearty laughter and some knee slapping erupted as "That just depends" concluded with a quick accordion run and the jingle of tambourine cymbals.

One group of dancers, gathered near Millie and Ollie, seemed to be particularly delighted by Reggie's off-color lyrics. A twittering voice rose from a woman at the center of the cluster, commanding everyone's attention, as did the low-cut black sheath dress she flaunted, which stood out against the ruffled blouses and flared skirts of other polka dancers.

As Reggie picked up the pace with his next lively tune, Millie took Ollie firmly by the arm and directed him off to another corner of the dance floor.

Snowplow Polka

"I saw you goggle-eye that Audrey Delcanto, Mr. Rolloff," Millie accused. "Why do all you men make such fools of yourselves around her?"

"I wasn't staring at anyone. I just heard that high-pitched laugh and wondered who it could be."

"You knew perfectly well it was Audrey. Every time she's around I see you looking at her. That blond is not her natural hair color, ya know, and all that pancake makeup hides a lot of wrinkles."

Ollie tried to reason with his partner. "Come on, Millie. Audrey is just a fun member of the group. I don't think about her that way, you're the only one for me."

After a few more dances, Ollie and Millie were eager to get back to their table. The festivities had begun so quickly that they hadn't had a chance to get a drink yet. Their friends had sprung for a few beers to toast the new business venture, and everyone was chortling about Reggie's knack for bringing out the best of times with his original tunes. Ollie loosened the slide of his bolo tie, which had a turquoise roadrunner set in coral. He opened the first pearl button of his western shirt and sat back looking satisfied. Nels Gustafson, sitting to his left, leaned in to be better heard.

"So, they finally shipped poor Swany back to the grapefruit league, eh?"

"Yah, his daughter lives in Bonita Springs, ya know," Ollie confirmed.

"I bet that means someone got a good deal on his plow truck."

Though delivered as a statement, Nels's question hung

there, but Ollie didn't want to show all his cards. These neighbors might expect a discount if they knew he'd gotten Swanson's truck for a song.

"I'd say Morty Mortensen at Mainz Motors can drive a pretty hard bargain," Ollie demurred. "Course I tried not to act too interested, but he knows I've wanted my own business for a long time. So I guess he held the winning hand."

"So you won't be given' no senior discounts?" Nels asked.

"Hell! That would be half the people on the route."

"Well at least we can be thankful that we'll have a driver who knows his way around."

"Darn tootin', Nels. I think the rates should be increased to reward the improved quality."

Nels paid no attention to that rebuttal but instead gathered a collection of napkins, beer coasters and stir sticks and began to lay them out on the shellacked table in a geometric pattern.

"Now here's the thing I want to show you—what Swany always got wrong." Nels navigated the tip of a stir stick between the pieces of the makeshift map he'd arranged. "Say this coaster here is the beginning of Richie's field, where QQ hits 2¼."

"His property don't go to 2¼, it ends at 2nd Street."

"No, it goes to 2¼. He plants potatoes in there every other year, when he ain't doin' corn."

"That isn't Richie's field, he just rents it from the DNR," Millie chimed in, speaking with authority about her brother's holdings. "That's DNR land all the way to the lake." She moved her finger along the coaster, then pointed off to some infinity mark beyond the table.

"OK," Nels conceded. "But you know the field I mean, right across from where my pasture starts . . ."

"That's your pasture?" Ollie looked closely at a napkin

Snowplow Polka

across from the first coaster. "Your pasture goes at that slight angle there where the county has a right of way for the drainage ditch." He lifted the napkin in question and refolded it with new creases to replicate the angles he'd mentioned.

"Looks good," Nels confirmed. "Now, up about a hundred feet is that last light pole." With his other hand, Nels took a swizzle stick and held its point at the spot where they were to imagine the utility. "Right after that pole is the roadway that leads to a metal swing gate on the backside of my north pasture. Now, Swany would never plow out that there road to the gate for me, and I pointed it out many times."

"That ain't no roadway, Nels." Ollie put his empty beer bottle aside and then noticed another full one already had taken its place. "That's just an unimproved gravel path that you use to move your cattle to the south forty across QQ. But you don't even use it all winter—the animals stay in the barn or at that other pasture by your trailer."

"Oh, you don't know everything I do with my animals, Ollie."

"And we don't wanna!" Millie hooted.

Embarrassed, Nels turned red, and his voice rose as he poked emphatically with his stir stick. "If that road ain't plowed all winter, it's so full of snow by spring that I can't open the gate until April. When the calves are born, I got to be able to move that herd. That road is a road, Ollie!"

"Don't blow a fuse, Nels." Ollie thought the neighbor's request was out of line, but knew this was exactly the kind of situation that defines how you do business. Besides, a good-sized crowd now formed a huddle around the table, and people were pointing at the patchwork map. "I can't be plowing an unused path every time it snows, but we'll make sure that walkway gets cleared before spring calving."

"That's what I want! Now that's a good plowman."

The assembly murmured its approval of this wise compromise.

Ollie and Millie had barely put back a self-congratulatory slug of beer when they saw Kenny and Myrtle Rudberg step forward, to air another grievance no doubt.

Kenny tried to locate his property in the bar paraphernalia on the table, but quickly realized that his home, being on Big Butternut Lake and not Little Butternut, wasn't represented. Instead, he refolded one napkin into a rough rectangle and presented it before the plowmeisters. "I need to explain why it's so hard for Myrtle and me to get out all winter, all cuz-a how backwards Swany always plowed our drive."

Ollie took a long swallow of his Honey Weiss and sat forward to ponder the riddle of the rectangle.

Kenny presented his case with an even voice. "Now, say this here's the driveway, and our garage door is on this side of the house. Well, all year, except winter, Myrt and I can back out of the garage, turn around just a little on the front lawn, then go forward right up the hill, slick as snot. So, when Swany did our drive, he never would clear the snow off that front yard spot so we could back up onto it. Instead, we had to go in reverse up our whole driveway. That's a dangerous thing in the winter, Ollie. We could end up in the ditch."

"So you want me to plow some of your front yard so's you can make that turn-around outside the garage?"

"That's right, by God! But you can't be scraping too low or you'll dig up the grass there like Swany did. I had to reseed the whole damn thing!"

"So Swany did plow there?"

"Well yah, once, but he did it so bad that I told him, 'Don't ever do that again.'"

Snowplow Polka

"So plow your front lawn by the drive, but not too close to the ground, very careful like?"

"That's it, you got the right idea, Ollie. Raise the blade just a bit, and also be sure the gravel from the driveway is off it, so those rocks aren't all piled on the lawn come spring."

"I'll be as careful as I can, Kenny." Ollie felt that this reassurance, combined with no specific promise, was a smart diplomatic move, defusing another hair-trigger client. When he heard Millie give a long sigh, he noticed that a small line had formed before them. Snow court was in full session.

By the time Reggie transitioned from the "Rock and Rye Polka" to a slow version of "Goodnight, Irene," Millie and Ollie realized that this traditional end-of-the-dance pairing meant that just about their whole evening had been spent doing business instead of dancing. Ollie was hoping that Millie had made mental notes to document their commitments. He felt that he had granted more favors then a Sicilian godfather at his daughter's wedding. Just as he was turning to his partner to suggest they glide off for the last few stanzas of the dance, a firm hand came down on his shoulder from behind. Ollie looked back and up to see the broad face of Sheriff Helmuth Trost looming above him.

"I'm glad I caught you."

It sounded casual enough, yet who wants to be "caught" by the police? Helmuth's big mitt stayed on Ollie's shoulder while his middle finger began an irritating tap.

"Will you be in town tomorrow to sign that contract at the village clerk's office?"

"Yah, yah sure, bright and early, soon as Lucille opens."

Geezer Power

Sheriff Trost bent over, cupped his hand by Ollie's ear and said, "I'll tell you the truth: I was hoping someone younger would take on the local plowing contract. We won't be disappointed, will we?"

"No, Helmuth—I mean, Sheriff. Hell no. We got the experience to compensate for not being so young, and we're always out of bed early."

"Will you have a partner, some backup?"

"Oh, Millie will be with me, ya know." Ollie touched her arm. "She's handled farm machinery her whole life."

"My husband, Virgil—his Harvester was the biggest in the township," Millie affirmed.

There was a long pause; the tapping finger kept time to the music. After a while, Helmuth released his grip, crouched like a football coach between the two seniors and gave them a conspiratorial look.

"Also, there's something I've been wanting to tell you." Helmuth's voice was nearly a whisper. "This cabin robber business that everyone's talking about? I gotta confess, it's got me worried."

Millie and Ollie leaned in a bit closer and watched as the sheriff rubbed his hands in a show of nerves.

"Near Riceland and all along the highway to Coopers Falls there's been trouble. These aren't just some local kids out looking for a place to party and crash. It looks more like professional crooks, and this wasn't the first time weapons were used."

Ollie felt as though he should be patting and consoling their distraught lawman. He looked over at Millie, and the concern in her eyes matched his own apprehension.

Helmuth drew a long breath. "No one has figured out who these guys are, but they seem to know the countryside pretty well, and a couple of things that were stolen have been fenced at pawn shops in the Cities."

"You don't think you've spotted them yet, eh Sheriff?" Millie asked.

"I think part of the problem is that it's too easy for them to spot me. When you drive around in a cruiser with lights on top and a sign on your door that says "Sheriff," you're not exactly hidden. A couple of times I saw some guys I wondered about, but so many people come out here in the winter to fish and snowmobile and check their cabins . . . I just can't stop every stranger for no reason."

"I get what you're thinking, Sheriff," said Ollie. "People like Millie and me driving around before a lot of tracks have been made in the snow might see something suspicious and be able to report it. We usually know who's here and who's not, so anyone different might stand out."

"You're reading my mind," Helmuth said with some relief. "Extra eyes out on the roads could help me put these criminals away. I can't officially deputize you two, but believe me, any help you can give law enforcement would be greatly appreciated."

"Goodnight, Irene" always ended with an audience sing-a-long, and the melancholy final verse had just concluded with the crowd's lament drifting off into the rafters.

Sheriff Trost stood up. "So I'll meet you bright and early at Lucille's office. They say there's snow in Montana tonight and it's on its way here."

They watched the policeman amble out the front door. "I sure as hell hope we can make a go of this," Ollie confessed, feeling a knot form in his guts.

"We're on probation, I'd say," Millie replied.

Geezer Power

From the small elevated platform that sufficed as a stage at the White Pines Tavern, Reggie seemed to detect the gloomy atmosphere that had descended on his friends' table. The crowd was now expecting his usual Sunday night benediction: "Auf Wiedersehen! We'll see you Wednesday at the VFW in Lichtenstein. Goodnight, sleep tight, and take out those dentures, so you won't bite." Instead, Reggie clapped his hands to get everyone's attention, "Folks, before you go, I'd like to recognize Millie Reinhart and Ollie Rolloff, this area's newest senior entrepreneurs. At an age when some folks would be packing it in and heading for the rest home, these kids are plowing snow and making greenbacks. I say we bring 'em out here on the floor and sing a round of 'I Ain't Goin' to the Home.'"

Then, to the tune of "It Ain't Gonna Rain No More," Reggie coaxed the familiar song from his accordion while shaking his percussive legwear in time.

> I ain't goin' to the Home. No way!
> I ain't goin' to the Home.
> Oh how in the heck would I get respect,
> If they put me in the Home?

At the conclusion of the first line, the dancers shouted "No way!" together and stomped their feet in sharp staccato on the floor. This rousing crowd pleaser sent the whole polka club out the door in a merry mood.

❄

The parking lot lights at the White Pine Tavern stayed on only long enough for the last dance group members to find their way back out to the road. As Ollie glanced at the driver's side mirror, he saw those beacons extinguish behind them and darkness close in all around.

There was an uncharacteristic hush in the Buick as it headed homeward to Little Butternut Lake through the moonless night.

Thoughtfully, Millie said, "I suppose the kids weren't completely off base when they were fretting about this cabin robber stuff. If Helmuth is actually worried, there must really be trouble. I'm going to keep my ears as cocked as a jackrabbit's."

"That was really something, that he as much as deputized us." Ollie beamed. "Heck, we're gonna be agents of the village."

This upbeat assessment didn't lift Millie's spirits much. "How can a road you've driven your whole life seem strange when you think something bad might be lurking in the woods? Why does it have to be so damn dark on winter nights up here?"

Cowbell Café

The Buick Park Avenue was back on the highway just six hours later, when the sun was making a valiant effort to force some golden shafts through a cloud bank.

"This is the calm before the storm," Ollie commented philosophically. "I can still see that last system behind us and now that next storm front is coming in from the west."

"I'm tired of this snowplowing business already," Millie replied, her voice a muffled drone seeping out of her down jacket. The diamond-patterned coat made her look like she'd rolled out of bed and taken the quilt along with her. "They haven't even signed our contract yet, but all we heard at the dance was customer complaints. Then we didn't get enough

Snowplow Polka

sleep; now we have to go into town early; and a blizzard's coming. Great business."

"Oh, don't be so gloomy, babe. This is gonna be great—just the break we needed. Remember how excited everyone was last night? They're all rooting for us."

"And they're all home sawing logs now," groused Millie, "while we're on the road earlier than the milkman, charging into Upper Mainz. Nothin' in town will even be open yet."

"The Cowbell Café is open. That's where all the business in town gets done anyway. I don't want Helmuth to say we were late, ya know."

Millie yawned. "I might just slip back to dreamland for a minute while you get us to this important meeting. At least the front seat of this Buick is almost as comfortable as our bed."

"That's right, we're riding in style," Ollie agreed, and then thought, *At least I get some support out of her for the car.* "These Park Avenues were one of the greatest cars ever made for keeping a steady pace on winter roads." As Ollie spoke, he glanced over to see Millie sinking into her overcoat, her head resting to the side. "She's low enough, wide enough, nice and hefty—it's like we're floating along the highway. You just nod off if ya want—you're cruising in the lap of luxury." Far ahead, the village started to come into view. The street lights were still on. Ollie patted the console of his sturdy ride and hummed a tune, then said, "Best winter vehicle ever, can't figure out why they ever stopped making 'em."

❄

To say the main street of Upper Mainz lasted four blocks was a bit of an exaggeration. The former creamery, long vacant, occupied most of the first block. At the other end of the street,

Cowbell Café

some wooden warehouse buildings that had serviced the railroad, back when the railroad went through town, were now rented out as storage units. The two blocks in between held what was left of the town's once thriving business district. A new business area had grown out along the highway, drawn away from Main Street by the need for more traffic, better parking and proximity to the casino.

True to Millie's prediction, there was hardly a car in town. Of course some of the business owners parked behind their buildings, but others parked right out on Main Street to make it look like there were customers at their stores. There were no lights on yet in the village clerk's office. Ollie prodded Millie awake, and they headed for the Cowbell, where a warm yellow light glowed behind steamed windows.

"I hope you made two extra donuts for some strangers in town!" Ollie flashed a smile toward the waitress as he shook himself out of his barn jacket and hung it next to Millie's coat on a hook by the door.

"Well I believe I did, since everyone in town knew you'd be here, *bright and early*," Cora, the café's owner, baker and waitress, declared. A metallic clang sounded from behind her, and the new arrivals looked at the pass-through window to the kitchen where Cora's husband, Adolph, gave a crooked half-smile and waved a shiny spatula in greeting. Adolph didn't like to talk much, since a stroke last year impaired his speech. Still, he knew how to cook the same as always, even if he now flipped hotcakes left-handed.

At the biggest table, stationed close to the front window, sat a small crowd of burghers, all of whom greeted or nodded their heads to Millie and Ollie as the new arrivals took seats at the counter. In a padded leather booth nearby, Pastor Skagen, from Moe Lutheran, was having breakfast with Father

Snowplow Polka

Dougherty, from Immaculate Conception Catholic Church. Some people in town thought their friendship kind of funny for competing shepherds, but the two obviously enjoyed talking to someone who knew what the heck the other one meant, and they would often be heard trying out sermon ideas on each other. Folks who had visited both venues said they could get about the same story at either one. The ministers nodded politely to the two lost sheep.

At a corner table near the front door, Rupert Everson, the owner, writer, editor and printer of the *Upper Mainz Rheinlander*, lifted a finger from his laptop in a quick hello. Rupert liked to maintain an appropriate distance from the other business owners in town so that his unbiased reporting would not be influenced by hearsay. More to the point, if he sat at the window table, people would constantly ask him to Google facts or sports scores they were arguing about. The corner table was his office away from the news desk.

Rupert wasn't the only patron on the clock that morning. Connie Smaland, the post office manager, was sorting through plastic USPS bins on one end of the crowded main table. She hated sitting in the post office across the street working by herself. There was hardly ever any foot traffic at her station, and if someone did arrive, she could run across the street and act as though she had just been out for a minute to get coffee. Connie had to have everything ready for Walter Bing to deliver by the time he was done with first milking. If he couldn't get the route done before evening milking, Walter would leave it for Connie to finish. The whole system worked pretty well except that the breakfast crew kept trying to peek at their neighbors' private correspondence while she sorted it, or else wanted to grab magazines they thought would be dirty because they had

Cowbell Café

brown wrappers. Connie had repeatedly told them these were punishable federal offenses.

"Hey Connie, are the Christmas stamps out yet?" asked Samuel Grittner, the drugstore owner and pharmacist.

"Any day now, Sam. I'll tell you first."

Vernon Nelson, the hardware store owner, nudged his friend. "Don't you mean *holiday* stamps?"

"No, I mean *Christmas*, damn it! It just don't feel right till I get those miniature pictures of Mary and baby Jesus each year. Makes me think I'm spreading the Good News with every card. Ain't that right, Pastor?" Sam shouted over his shoulder to the clergy table.

"We appreciate your assistance, Samuel," Jens Skagen answered mildly. "But we also pray that your language will stay as pure as your heart."

"Jesus, you're right, Jens. I should be more careful with my swearing. After all, there's ladies present."

"And servants of the Lord."

"And agents of the federal government," Connie said.

"And newspaper reporters," Rupert added.

"We are always being watched over, Samuel," concluded Pastor Skagen.

The whole gathering nodded amen to that truthful lesson. Before another piece of wisdom could be submitted for consideration, Adolph, at the kitchen pass-through, gestured urgently for attention and put great effort into saying "Lu, Lu, Lucille!" as he pointed his spatula toward the café's front window.

Ollie saw the village clerk's Chevy Blazer turn onto Main and park in its reserved space. Lucille Carlson climbed out and then waddled toward the public safety building at what was, for her, a swift pace.

Snowplow Polka

"Wish me luck, folks!" Ollie spoke with a flourish as he slid off the stool. "When I come back you'll have to make room for me at the big window table—I'll be a businessman."

Everyone shouted their support and then watched with amusement as the excited man alternately picked up and put down his coffee mug and strawberry glazed donut while struggling into his barn jacket. Then he raced for the door.

"Millie, ain't you goin'?" Cora asked.

"Nope, this is Ollie's part of the business."

❄

"Lucille, Lucille! We've been here for a while waiting for you and the sheriff," Ollie shouted from across the street as he hurried to catch the village clerk while still fighting to get his right arm through the coat sleeve. The greeting didn't make Lucille stop and wait, but she at least held up a finger to acknowledge she'd heard him, before disappearing into the building.

When the breathless man reached the door, his right hand finally punched out from the canvas sleeve just in time to grab the handle. Ollie looked at the remnants of the squashed jelly donut still clenched in his fist.

"Oops! Jeez, what a mess," he said as he watched a sticky web of red goo stretch between his fingers.

Passing through the vestibule and entering the main office, he saw that Lucille was bent over her desk, talking on the phone.

"I know, I know, Helmuth. I got here as quickly as I could. Have you contacted the Riceland Police Department yet? I think they've probably got a backup squad they can send. I know they have a good photographer, too." She was frowning and nervously shifting her weight from one foot to the other.

Cowbell Café

Ollie got the feeling he might not be seeing the sheriff that day.

"Where are the Rudbergs now?" Lucille sounded rattled. "Will they be staying with her cousin over in Lichtenstein? Can they drive themselves?"

"The Rudbergs?" Ollie whispered. He could hardly believe what he was overhearing. He had just talked to them last night. They lived over by Big Butternut Lake. That was right in the neighborhood. "What's wrong?"

Lucille waved her hand to shush Ollie.

"What about telling the people in town?" she asked the sheriff. "Is this something you want to keep a lid on?" She paused, listening, and then said, "I'm sure all the regulars are at the Cowbell, as usual. OK, OK, call my cell if you need me. Good luck."

With a deep sigh Lucille hung up the phone. "Oh . . . Ollie, we've had an emergency." Then she noticed her friend's jelly-filled palm. "My goodness, look at your hand. Can I get you a paper towel?"

"Oh yah, thanks. I just had a little accident with a donut. But it sounds like there's worse news coming this way. I heard you mention the Rudbergs, are they alright?"

"They're alright, just shook up. It looks like another robbery, but this time it wasn't a closed cabin, it was a year-round home. Kenny and Myrtle were only out for the evening at the White Pines."

"They were at the dance last night!" the startled man exclaimed. "They were standing right in front of me, big as life, and we had a real good talk."

"They're not dead, Ollie! Oh, this is so disturbing. These thieves are getting bolder all the time! It looks like none of us is safe."

Snowplow Polka

"Yup, this is bad news. I can keep a secret if you want me to. I'm almost a village employee, as soon as you sign my snowplow contract."

"I've got the contract right here, but I can't notarize it without a witness. I thought the sheriff would be here to do that."

She clicked off the desk lamp and buttoned her car coat. "Let's get over to the Cowbell. Helmuth thinks it's better if as many people as possible know about this right away."

❄

"Here they come, here they come! Get ready to clap!" Vern Nelson exclaimed.

"They don't look so happy," Sam Grittner said as he rubbed condensation off the window with the sleeve of his pharmacist's jacket and watched the approaching pair.

"Not happy?" asked Millie.

Cold air rushed into the café, and the buzz of excitement was quickly squelched as Lucille and Ollie entered with troubled looks.

"The Rudbergs' house was robbed!" Lucille exclaimed.

"Helmuth's there now," Ollie added.

"A backup squad is on its way," Lucille gasped as she tried to catch her breath. "Oh, this is just awful!"

"Cora, please get Lucille a cup of coffee," Pastor Skagen said as he beckoned the village clerk to join him on the bench seat at the minister's booth.

Father Dougherty reached over the table and offered Lucille his hand in comfort.

"What time did the crime take place?" Rupert Everson asked while typing.

Cowbell Café

"Before midnight," the anxious clerk said. "They were only at the White Pines Tavern for the Sunday night dance."

"That's not late at all!" Sam sputtered. "May and I were at that dance, too. Hell, this could have happened to any of us."

Vern summed up the group's anxiety: "These guys must know just what we're doing. This village is being watched!"

"Yah, a watcher," Sam said. "I wonder if it could be that creepy Amos Nedahammer. He always seems to be watching from the woods."

"Now don't go calling Amos a creep, Sam," Millie interjected. "He's been our neighbor his whole life."

"You can't tell me he isn't out there creeping around. Isn't that what 'creep' means?"

"His habits may seem peculiar," said Connie Smaland, "but we shouldn't be calling him names like that. Sometimes, when I have to finish Walter's route and it's getting dark, it makes me feel kinda good to know he's out there. Amos isn't just watching, it's more like he's watching over us."

"Amos is a veteran," Rupert pointed out. "God knows a lot of good guys never come back the same from a war."

"His knowledge of scripture is really quite admirable," added Pastor Skagen, in defense of the hermit of Upper Mainz. "I doubt that I could quote from the Book of Amos as well as he can."

"One thing's for sure," Ollie concluded. "I don't think he'd be hiding any stolen goods in his screwy shack. I'll bet it's already packed full of junk."

The whole group chuckled at this summation of their eccentric neighbor. With the subject of Amos Nedahammer put to rest, everyone again prodded Lucille for information.

"The sheriff is mighty worried!" Lucille blurted. "Guns

Snowplow Polka

were taken! Kenny had a rifle, a shotgun and pistol, and ammo, too. They're all gone, all in the hands of criminals."

Father Dougherty patted Lucille's hand one more time, slid out of the booth, and wrestled into his long topcoat, excusing himself. "Kenneth and Myrtle are in my congregation. I have to go check on them. They need my support at a time like this."

"They're at her cousin's in Lichtenstein," the clerk told him. "The Rudberg's home is now a crime scene. Who's next?" Lucille started to shudder at this thought and blotted a tear with a Kleenex.

"I've gotta get to my hardware store," Vern said as he zipped up his parka. "They're going to be needing things."

Connie stacked her mail bins and also headed toward the door. "I'll warn Walter. Maybe he'll see something while he's on the route. Oh, I'm worried for him all alone out there."

Next, Rupert joined the exodus. He clicked his laptop shut and declared, "Now I've gotta rearrange my whole Wednesday edition. This is the new lead article for sure, unless they catch those bastards. That's a story I'd love to print!"

"Better tell them to hold the presses, Rupert," Sam said as he watched him leave.

"You know darn well I'm the pressman, too," Rupert replied with exasperation as the door shut behind him.

"Humph," Cora exhaled, surveying the nearly deserted café. "I guess anytime I need to clear the joint out, I'll give you a call, Lucille." She put her arm around the still shaking clerk while Pastor Skagen did the same from the other side. "You just stay right here, sweetheart. I bet you haven't even had any breakfast yet. Sit with Pastor Skagen and drink your coffee and try to relax. Adolph's going to cook you a special three-cheese omelet."

Cowbell Café

There was nothing more to learn and not much to say among the remaining Cowbell patrons. Before long, Millie and Ollie also bid their farewells and headed back out to the Buick.

"Now that was a bit more excitement than we counted on," Ollie said.

Millie sighed. "I suppose the contract never got signed."

We're Plowin' Now!

"Ollie, Ollie! Get the dang phone!"

The startled man snapped to a seated position with the force of a spring-loaded trap.

"I can't, I can't! I got to pee!" he squealed while ripping back the bed covers. Before Ollie's feet even hit the floor, a charley horse gripped the calf of his right leg, causing him to wince and whimper all the way to the bathroom.

Millie got a quick glimpse of his gimpy exit as she patted the bed stand to find her reading glasses. "Who would be calling us at 6:30 a.m.? 6:30! I thought I told you to set the clock for 5:00!" she yelled at her hobbling lover while Tammy Wynette sang "My Elusive Dreams" in the background.

Snowplow Polka

Millie composed herself for a moment. Then she threw a slipper in the direction of the bathroom. "Quit whining and shut the door!" She rolled to Ollie's side of the bed to slap the snooze button on the clock radio and reach for the ringing phone.

Picking up the receiver, she tried to feign a breezy air. "Hello?"

"Millie? Is that you?" The woman's voice, an exaggerated whisper peppered with fear, was nearly unintelligible.

"Yes," Millie replied, finding herself whispering back. *Why is she talking like that?* Lucille's panicked tenor lent an atmosphere of crisis to the dialogue.

"Where are you two?" the village clerk asked desperately. "We always try to have our plows on the road by 5:30. Oscar Nielsen has already left a message about his driveway!" The last words were delivered with a screeching pitch that sounded like air escaping a balloon.

Tell the truth or lie? Millie decided to take a chance with the truth. Maybe their new business was just too darn much work for an elderly couple, after all.

"Ollie must have hit the snooze button before I heard it. I'm sorry Lucille, we're moving now. We'll be on the road in ten minutes."

"Oooh, please hurry!" the clerk urged. "I told the sheriff I was sure you two could do this job. I can count on you, right?"

"We're on duty, Lucille!"

Millie slammed the phone down. She jumped out of bed, took off her flannel nightgown and flung it in a twisted heap on a chair, grabbed her bathrobe, charged across the bedroom, and shoved open the bathroom door. There she encountered Ollie, still bent over, massaging his calf.

We're Plowin' Now!

"Stick those knobby legs into some pants and get downstairs and start the truck!" she barked. "No shaving and no breakfast. What the heck happened to the clock radio?" She grabbed her toothbrush.

"The radio came on, but it didn't seem to wake me," he said, moving toward the sink. "I was havin' a dream. We were dancing at the White Pines, but then it changed to somewhere else. The floors weren't wood anymore, they were marble and there was this huge chandelier. Oh, it was just beautiful."

Ollie kept talking, his words garbled, as he brushed his teeth. "Oh, yah, and Tammy Wynette was singing there."

"In your dreams, Ollie!" Millie said, sputtering toothpaste bubbles. "Why didn't you set that darn clock to alarm instead of radio? I suppose you'd rather hear Tammy Wynette than get to work on time?"

They nearly bumped heads as both bent over at the same instant to spit into the sink.

Millie looked at her haggard reflection in the mirror and shrugged; there wouldn't be time for lipstick, eyebrow pencil or curling her gray hair. *Now, what to wear?* Sweatpants and T-shirt under a snowmobile suit seemed like they would fit the bill. Descending the staircase, she heard the microwave ding. "Are you warming up coffee? I told you not to do that! Oscar Nielsen already phoned Lucille about his driveway. Make me a cup too." She looked at her disheveled partner and gave him a quick peck on his whiskers. "I guess I have to stand by my man. Grab your travel mug, Ollie, it's plow time!"

❄

In their empty bedroom the clock radio clicked back on and an announcer with a deep, friendly voice broadcast his greetings.

Snowplow Polka

"Good morning, Lake Country, and all of you Northland listeners. I hope you've been enjoying our Tammy Wynette marathon this a.m. No teardrops in the milking pail, I hope. Now let's get on to that crop report while we dig ourselves out of last night's seven-inch snowfall."

❄

Ollie briskly swept snow from the truck with a long-handled broom while Millie shoveled their walkway. The plow truck would just barely fit in the garage, and Ollie hadn't cleaned out enough space for it yet, so it was still parked in the driveway and had to be excavated from a snowdrift. The driver's door groaned on its hinges as Ollie pried it open. *Even trucks don't like to sleep out all night in a Wisconsin snowstorm*, he mused.

The vinyl seat felt like a slab of ice. But the F-250 had been outfitted with an engine block heater, and Ollie had remembered to drag an extension cord out from under the garage door and plug in the truck. *Thank God for that!*

Even with this pre-heating, the monster engine was none too eager to turn over. It gave a cranky growl, like a hibernating bear being prodded with a stick. But in a heaving shudder, at last the Ford roared to life. Millie hopped up into the passenger seat and gave her partner's mitten-covered hand a slap.

"Let's plow some snow, old man!"

Ollie flipped on the radio to catch the end of the crop projections—once a farmer always a farmer. He turned his head around, dropped the truck into reverse, threw his arm over the backseat and looked out the rear window. As they eased away from the garage, he heard Millie snarl, "Jesus, Mary and Joseph above!"

We're Plowin' Now!

Ollie, turned forward again to find the reason for the blessing, but didn't notice anything wrong at first. Then it struck him—the truck was crunching backwards, but the plow blade was still sitting stoically in front of the garage door. *I forgot to connect the damn blade!*

The cab immediately seemed to get a whole lot hotter, and Ollie felt Millie's eyes cutting a hole through the fur of his rabbit skin hat. "I was gonna hook that blade up last night," the flustered driver explained. "Morty said you should do it in daylight to make sure the pins fall into the right place. It was already dark when we got home last night, so I guess I forgot."

There was no need at all for Millie to criticize this weak excuse; it already hung there, as lame as a three-legged dog. All she said, spitting each word out like a hot bolt from a rivet gun, was, "Where are the pins?"

"They're right here behind the seat."

Ollie eased the Ford back to the garage, trying hard to align the frame on the front of the truck with the brackets on the blade's connection struts. The protruding tongues on the frame would slide right into notches on the struts if he could just get them aligned perfectly. *Closer . . . Closer . . . Yes!*

The docking looked great. Now if only the clevis pins would drop correctly through the aligned holes. Ollie climbed out from the high cab and then felt behind the seat for the box of pins. He tried to assure himself that everything would fit properly as he cautiously approached the conjoined pair. Morty had said the pins were a little hard to get lined up. The salesman suggested that they might have to be shaken some before they dropped all the way into position. Ollie didn't relish the idea of sharing these details with Millie. He yanked off a deerskin mitten and blew breath into his cupped hand to

Snowplow Polka

keep it warm for the delicate maneuver. Just as he was carefully positioning his hand in order to place the connector, the F-250's horn gave an ear-splitting blare. The pin shot away from his fingers and dove into the snow.

"Will you just put the damn things in!" yelled Millie as she stuck her head out the truck window.

Ollie saw the impression in the snow where the stray pin had landed. He winced and felt around in the frigid fluff with his bare hand. *There it is.* He snagged the pin and dropped it into place. Sure enough, instead of going in completely, the pin fell partway and then refused to go further. The second pin stuck too, swaying in its socket like a crab's eye rotating on its stalk.

"Get a hammer!" Millie shouted, craning her head out the window and pumping her fist.

That might work. Ollie got a nice ball-peen hammer from his truck toolbox and started tapping the stubborn stakes, holding them in place to avoid more airborne missiles. Graduating from taps to whacks, his frustration rising, Ollie realized he would now have to resort to the shake method described by Morty.

"You call that hammering?"

Ollie got back into the cab, bracing for more of his partner's barbs.

"Morty showed me this trick. If we just shake the blade some, those babies will drop down and then I'll be able to get the cotter pins into them."

"Shake the blade?"

"Yah, I'll need you to get out and let me know when the pins drop in place."

Ollie cautiously worked the blade's hydraulic lift lever. He raised it just slightly, and next reversed the direction with a

We're Plowin' Now!

flick of the wrist, then gave it an upward twist and another quick drop.

As Millie watched, the half-set pins rolled precariously in the depressions, but then, as if by divine intervention, they fell firmly into their slots. She gave Ollie a thumbs up.

"That's what I'm talking about!" the jolly plowman cried. He hopped out from the rumbling Ford and ran over to secure the cotter pins. He was grinning from ear to ear as they climbed back into the cab.

Ollie knew Millie wasn't about to congratulate him. *She probably thinks this whole production was a waste of precious time.* He raised the blade a bit and got ready to back up again. His half-numb fingers, searching for the gear, instead dropped the vehicle into low. Simultaneously, his wet boot slipped on the floor mat and skidded onto the accelerator. The F-250 jumped forward, like a football player off the line, and charged the garage door. Ollie stomped on the brakes and reached for the transmission knob, but his hand instead hit the plow blade's hydraulic lift lever. The mighty steel blade fell to the ground with a tooth-shattering crash, nearly lifting the truck's rear wheels off the driveway. Ollie and Millie jerked forward against their seatbelts, then back against the brittle vinyl headrests.

The two were dumbfounded—no exclamations, no curses, no crying, just the open-mouthed frozen expressions of two near-victims who had felt the reaper's scythe sing past their heads.

Millie looked wide-eyed at Ollie as he gradually moved the shifter back toward Park in millimeter increments. A person carrying nitroglycerin could not have been more cautious. When the metallic click signaled safety, they looked at the closed garage door looming in front of them. It was close enough to fill the entire windshield.

Snowplow Polka

Ollie descended from the cab to check for damage. Even in his clunky boots he felt like he was tiptoeing. The massive plow blade, built to shear through ice dams, would have crushed the aluminum door like paper. Yet what to his wondering eyes should appear? Four slivers of paint that had been shaved off, but not a single dent in the door. Ollie, leaning on one knee, sighted the length of the plow. Light could barely pass between the steel guillotine and the garage door, but there was no real damage.

Whooooof, that was close. He breathed a sigh of relief.

"Even a blind chick sometimes finds a kernel of corn," Ollie said, and winked at Millie as he got back in the cab.

❄

Ascending the driveway, Ollie practiced raising and lowering the blade in small steps to find the exact height that would graze the loose gravel but not dig it up. When he was satisfied that the position was just right, he looked at the lever projecting from the lift housing to memorize how it should be placed. To his astonishment, there was a deep scratch mark cut into the box indicating the exact same height he had just calculated. *That Swany wasn't completely nuts*, he thought.

As the truck crested the hilltop where their property met 2¼, they paused and looked out over a never-ending ocean of white.

"Where's the road?" Ollie wondered aloud.

"I don't know," Millie replied, trying to keep a straight face. "The road's always plowed when we get here."

"Who the hell was supposed to plow this?" Ollie sputtered.

They looked at one another and shook with laughter. After they composed themselves, Millie got out her clipboard to

We're Plowin' Now!

review the client roster and the list of roads assigned to them. Ollie recited the priorities Helmuth had stipulated: "Our first obligation is to the minor residential and service roads and then move on to the private drives."

"The road has no curves here," Millie noted. "Angle the blade to the right, look for the midpoint between power poles and fences, and watch the shoulder as we go." Her logical plan of attack reassured Ollie, and he dropped the blade to the slightly lower scratch mark, which he figured had to indicate blacktop level, and pointed the truck toward 2¼ Street.

"Yah! We're plowin' now!" Millie cheered.

Between tracking the side of the road beneath the blade, watching for any oncoming traffic and seeing where the plow's wake landed, Ollie felt like he needed a third eye.

"I'm going to try looking ahead—you watch where the wake is going. We don't want to be like Swany and wipe out any mailboxes."

When they got to the intersection with 14½, Ollie asked, "Should we do the first side of 14½ now, or turn around and do the other side of 2¼?"

"14½ first. If we do the other side of 2¼ we'll be back where we started with only one road done."

"We could clear the windrows from the shoulder on our second run back along here."

"Windrows? We'll finish the shoulders later, Mister Fancy-Plow-Words."

When they arrived at the County Road K stop sign they encountered the first clear pavement that had already been plowed by one of the township trucks. These oversized vehicles always left behind a treacherous ridge of snow chunks along the side of the road, blocking access to all the private drives.

Snowplow Polka

"Now we'll take K to 15th Street and clear the service road over there that we've been assigned," said Millie.

Off to the right, on the driveway to Johnson's farm, a figure in the distance caught Ollie's attention. It was Johnny Johnson waving his arms frantically.

As Ollie drove the truck forward, Johnny switched to wind-milling swoops that beckoned them to enter his drive. "Maybe it's an emergency—do you think someone's hurt?"

"The Johnsons aren't on the plow list," Millie said tentatively as she flipped through paperwork on the clipboard. "Nope," she confirmed. "I bet he just wants us to clear that ridge blocking his driveway."

"Should I get Helmuth on the CB to see if they called 911?" Ollie asked.

"Are you batty? The first thing he'll ask is how far we've gotten."

"I won't leave a neighbor in trouble. Besides, Helmuth said we're like deputized village workers now."

Millie rolled her eyes at the thought of how this job had inflated Ollie's self-image. "Why don't you raise the blade so they don't get a free plowing out of us?" she grumped.

"Don't be cruel, babe."

The plow threw a beautiful crescent plume of white as they broke through the icy ridge and drove toward Johnny Johnson, who continued to signal them forward and then switched to the repetitious pantomime of an airport grounds worker directing a jumbo jet into position. As they rounded the circular drive, past the barn and garage, Johnny's hands switched to small nudging and cautionary signs that eased the truck to the steps of his porch.

"What's wrong?" Ollie asked, as he lowered his window.

We're Plowin' Now!

Johnny spoke breathlessly. "Oh golly! Florence forgot to send in our money to Lucille and I never woulda gotten out of this drive without it being plowed."

"Some emergency," Millie fumed.

"Why didn't you renew your contract?" Ollie asked.

"Oh, we didn't have a contract last year. We was kinda hoping it wouldn't snow so much this winter, but this is kinda an emergency, especially for early November."

Is he really that dumb, or is he just hoping I am? thought Ollie.

Johnny managed to keep a slack-jawed Barney Fife expression on his mug. "Swany was always good about helping me out. I'd slip him a few bucks and he'd do my drive without needin' no contract."

"How many bucks?" Millie leaned over onto her driver and fixed the farmer with a steely glare.

"Ah, oh, ten bucks? He'd just do what you're doin', come down and turn around in the drive and head on out again, no harm done."

"Well, Johnny, we ain't no Swany. Why do you think he slipped off to Florida?" Millie's voice was as tough as her gaze. "We'll take the ten bucks this time, but you better contact Lucille and get on the roster."

Johnny made a show of fishing about in his Carhartt overalls, but came up empty-handed. "My money must be in my other pants," he admitted sheepishly.

No further words were needed. Ollie got the truck in gear and took off so quickly that Johnny had to jump backwards onto his front porch.

Even over the roar of the accelerating diesel engine, Millie's departing jab rang out loud and clear. "Mail me the sawbuck, you skinflint Swede!"

Snowplow Polka

While he closed his window, Ollie swore. "Now I *am* gonna raise the blade."

"Don't be cruel, babe."

❄

Cutting a smooth swath on the service road past 15th, Ollie and Millie had almost made it to High Cedar Road, the farthest point on the route, when they encountered more trouble. It was just before this intersection that the Nielsens' driveway met the service road. Ollie and Millie had been praying that they could fly by this hazard, even though they knew Oscar had telephoned Lucille before they had even gotten out of bed. Lo and behold, there was Oscar Nielsen himself, at the end of his property, pretending to be hanging a Christmas wreath on his mailbox. He turned around as the truck approached, feigning surprise at an unanticipated encounter. He raised his hand, palm forward, in a sign that he wanted to talk, and the plow ground to a halt. Approaching the driver's side window, the elderly customer spoke in a pleading voice.

"Do you think you could plow out my drive, Ollie, so I can get into town?"

Ollie and Millie exchanged glances, figuring Oscar had no good reason to go into town right that minute. He was just as retired as they were and could certainly put off any voyage until later. Yet, this presented a ticklish situation. Oscar's retirement hobby was ranting about shoddy public services, whining about tax hikes and haunting village board meetings to report on unfair and discriminatory treatment around the community.

"We'd love to help out, Oscar," Ollie began diplomatically, "but our first obligation is to the minor residential and service

We're Plowin' Now!

roads, and then we can do the private drives." You wouldn't want to disappoint the other tax payers would you?" *Huh. Bureaucratic hierarchy can be pretty handy,* Ollie mused.

"Oh, you know I'd hate to be a bother. Still, I was expecting the road to be done about an hour ago, so I was thinkin' you'd be back to do my drive by this time already."

Millie affected a neighborly air. "Where ya'll heading to, the post office? I know for a fact that those Christmas stamps aren't in yet."

"I don't think a private citizen's business in town is the affair of anyone else around here. Maybe I was just goin' to deliver a letter to the editor of the *Rheinlander* about the quality of village services here in Upper Mainz."

Check and mate, thought Ollie. He backed carefully to get a good clean angle on the Nielsons' entry without getting too near the fence. After cleanly cutting a series of parallel rows over Oscar's large parking area, he went back to finish off the small remaining trails that the plow had left. Ollie then cautiously approached the garage and dropped the blade to back-drag the drifts away from the doors. In the rear-view mirror Oscar could be seen back at the mailbox, his figure outlined by the rising sun. The man's shadow was cast along the length of the driveway and hung upon their work. Coming back up the drive, Millie rolled down her window to hear what the farmer was saying as he pointed to some barely visible lumps by the intersection with the road.

"Watch out for those decorative rocks here at the end of the drive. Come right next to them, but don't knock 'em out of place."

I should be using a whisk broom, not a truck, thought Ollie. He aligned the plow and crept toward the near-invisible landmarks. The blade shaved so close that the remaining thin veil

Snowplow Polka

of snow collapsed and fell away from the nearest boulder. Oscar actually gave a nod and grunt of approval to this microsurgery. Then—with no thanks, smile or goodbye—he raised his hand almost imperceptibly in dismissal and marched back toward his barn.

The truck had been outfitted with a bullhorn, which was bolted to the hood, allowing the driver to broadcast warnings to inattentive citizens or livestock. Millie bent over, depressed the thumb switch on the microphone and shouted, "Dummkopf!"

The vulgar rebuke echoed across the frozen field. Oscar flinched and spun around with a shocked expression. Millie's window was still open, and with false innocence she tittered, "I was talking to Ollie. I didn't know that darn thing was turned on."

Millie left it on, and the indignant landowner heard crackling laughter from the bullhorn as the snowplow sped off toward High Cedar Road.

❄

When their obligations to the village had been completed, Ollie began to work on the private properties that had contracts. He was eager to do this work as quickly and cleanly as possible. There was some real satisfaction in seeing other neighbors, people he actually liked, wave appreciatively as the plow broke through the roadside slush ridge and swept in to clear paths to the snowbound homes. It still burned him that the two private drives he had done first were those of the swindler Johnny Johnson and the carper Oscar Nielsen. But the goodwill of other customers had now lightened his mood.

The rhythm of the plowing, the brilliant morning sun and

We're Plowin' Now!

the vast sparkling blanket of white snow had a hypnotic effect on the plow team. Silence descended upon the truck's cab as Ollie methodically took care of each driveway and Millie checked them off the clipboard list.

Into this peaceful atmosphere, Ollie said, "I just figured it out."

"Figured what out?" asked Millie, "You can't tell me you figured Oscar Nielsen out, or they'd give you one of them psychiatrist degrees."

"No, I meant my dream, that ballroom I was telling you about earlier this morning. I remembered where that was."

Millie wasn't very interested in hearing anymore about his fantasies that had made them late for work, but she managed a noncommittal "Yah?"

"We were dancing in the ballroom of the Empress Hotel. Do you recollect how beautiful that floor was there, black-and-white tiles that spiraled around? We really should reserve that place for our Christmas dance next year."

"The Empress? You mean in Superior?"

"Yah, yah right downtown!"

"Ollie, they demolished that abandoned hotel years ago. Didn't you know that?"

"Oh, no," he sighed. "How could they have done that? They'll never build another ballroom like that again."

"So we were dancing there, eh, babe? What else was goin' on in your dream?"

"Oh, uhh . . . there was more, but you know just silly things that pop into your head at night. Who knows where they come from."

"What kind of silly things, Mr. Rolloff?" prodded Millie.

"You know, we were talking, laughing, with people from the dance club, stuff like that."

Snowplow Polka

"Laughing, huh? Who were you laughing with?" This sounded suspicious to Millie, like there might have been beautiful things in this dream other than just floor tiles.

Ollie shrugged off the question and gave a casual dismissal. "The whole polka club was there."

"It couldn't have been Audrey Delcanto, with the giddy laugh and those candy-apple lips, could it?"

The blushing driver tried to act as if the drifted snow took his complete attention, staring at the road rather than at his interrogator.

"Oh you men are all such dips!" Millie huffed. "Audrey! That blond hussy with the silly dress that's too tight for polka dancing! I bet that's what you're really looking for, eh? Go ahead, ask her out. I hear she won't say no."

"Oh Millie, come on," Ollie pleaded. "Who knows why you have wacky thoughts while you're dreaming." He put his hand on her well-insulated leg and spoke reassuringly. "You're the only one for me, honey. That's why we're together, right? Can you imagine Audrey out here zipped up in a snowmobile suit and plowing roads?"

That doesn't sound like much of a compliment, Millie thought, *but I do like being out here in the plow with the old coot.* Looking over at her man, she saw him frowning. Then the F-250 slowed to a crawl.

"Did you see a deer or something?" she asked and looked off to the right to where Ollie was staring.

"No, I saw some tire tracks going into the rest stop entrance back there but no tracks on the exit side." A line of tall Scotch pines shielded the retreat from the highway. Ollie checked his mirrors, then dropped the truck into reverse and backed up to the rest stop entrance. "This is supposed to be closed for the season, but look, the chain isn't in place."

We're Plowin' Now!

"That chain's been unhooked for months," Millie pointed out. "Kids go in there to make out. We got to keep rolling, Ollie. We're gettin' even more behind."

The driver lifted off his fur hat and scratched his matted hair. "Hmm . . . I think we should check it out. Something might be wrong."

"We're not gonna plow in there, though. It's a seasonal facility and not on our route."

"I'm not plowing, just looking," Ollie said, and rolled the truck toward the parking area near the closed facilities. The single set of tracks led to a rusted older model Chevy Impala that had parked alongside the pine trees in a truck space to avoid having to back up when it left.

Ollie slowly approached the passenger side of the sedan and looked down into it from the plow truck's high cab.

"Hmm . . . the windows are all steamed, and I can tell someone's inside," he said in a voice that dropped to a near whisper. "Probably sleeping."

"Right, sleeping it off I'll bet," Millie said while propping herself on the steering wheel to look out his window. "You know what they say about letting sleeping dogs lie."

"Yah, but they shouldn't be in here and we're practically village agents now." Ollie reached for his door handle.

"Do *not* get out of this truck!"

Ollie instead grabbed the bullhorn's microphone and hailed the other vehicle. "Ahoy, the Impala. Are you alright?" Getting no response, he gave the truck's horn a quick tap and repeated his message.

This got a reaction. A hand inside the car began to rub the condensation off the window. A skinny guy who had been lying on the front seat, shook his head and with a dazed expression, looked up at Ollie.

Snowplow Polka

This is no local kid, Ollie thought. He extended his right arm back across Millie's chest in a gesture of warning, hoping she would understand his concern. He turned to meet her eyes, and she made it clear she got his point.

The Chevy bounced slightly as the guy shifted over to the driver's side and turned on the ignition. Slowly the rear window facing the truck slid open. A middle-aged man with a ruddy complexion squinted from under the brim of a waxed canvas hunting hat.

Ollie opened his window, too. His elevated perch gave him a pretty good view into the Impala, and he was sure that the long cases lying on the back floor of the car surrounded by empty bottles and fast food wrappers were gun cases. *Rifles. Huh. Hunting season is over, though.*

"Good morning," the man yawned, stretching and scratching in a display that might have been too theatrical. The stench of alcohol and stale cigarette smoke wafted from the open window. "What time is it?"

Ollie saw a watch on the man's wrist, but still responded. "Almost noon. This rest area is closed for the season. You gotta get moving."

"Sure, sure, thanks for the wake-up call, mister," the man replied. "We didn't want to break the law. We just needed a place to stop and sleep."

That sounded innocent enough, but Ollie thought these guys should disclose a little more information. "I haven't seen you around here before. Are you just passing through?"

"Yah. We're on our way to Duluth." The man yawned again. "Got jobs waiting for us on an ore boat."

"We've been having some trouble in this area," Ollie said. "Homes been broken into. The sheriff asked me to keep a watch out for suspicious activity, ya know what I mean?"

We're Plowin' Now!

"Yah, I know what you mean. Anything can happen out here, but we're just passing through," the man in the canvas hat replied.

I'm done talking to this character, thought Ollie. "Good luck with the job. I gotta get plowin'."

He rolled up the window and murmured to Millie, "Turn around and get that car's plates. We're going to call this in to the sheriff."

❅

The man in the backseat got out, walked around to the driver's side and grunted, "Move over Jedidiah, we gotta hit the road."

"Damn! That snoop seen us real good, Hank." The high-strung younger guy swore. "I bet he'll report us. And it looked like there was two of 'em in that cab."

"Now we gotta dump this car," grumped Hank. "That geezer's gonna keep sniffing around. Witnesses like that can put a crimp in our operation."

Blood of the Lamb

"It's two o'clock, I'm dog tired, and I'm starving," moaned Millie.

"We haven't eaten all day, nothing but two mugs of coffee—we're driving on empty," added Ollie. "Thank God we're almost home. What have we got to eat there?"

"Nothing, remember? Last night we ate all the leftovers from Sunday when the kids were here.

Ollie looked hungrily at a herd of Black Angus as they drove past Richie's pasture. "I wish I could run right over and take a bite out of that one's butt."

"I know what ya mean," Millie seconded. "My stomach thinks my head's been cut off. Wait, wait, Amos's mailbox is just ahead. He never collects the papers, they just pile up. I want

Snowplow Polka

to check something out that could get us a quick free meal."

"Are you sure you want to borrow something from Nedahammer's mailbox? We've already had one close encounter with oddballs today." Ollie fidgeted as he looked at the overgrown driveway leading into Amos's property. "I don't want to annoy the recluse. For God's sake, have you ever seen his place? It's covered in flattened beer kegs! Didn't you say the Nedahammer's home used to be a regular farmhouse when his parents were still alive?"

"Yah, it never was much more than a log cabin painted white. His mom and dad had a few dairy cows but the land was too rocky to be any good, and now the barn has completely rotted away. Just pull over, would you? I know Amos and he knows me. It ain't his fault that when he got back from Nam he weren't normal."

As the snowplow ground to a halt, Millie reached out to grab the most recent edition of the *Rheinlander* from Amos's newspaper box. The container was as neatly stuffed with rolled papers as an untouched pack of cigarettes. She figured the least yellowed copy would be the latest. Rattling the sheets open, she flipped to the last inside page.

"Hurry, Millie," Ollie squirmed. "I can see some flickering light through the trees."

"That's just sunlight bouncing off his beer-keg siding."

"How the hell did he get all those kegs?"

"One of his army buddies who works for Leinenkugel's drops off used ones that are meant to be recycled. Amos cuts 'em apart and pounds 'em flat."

"Humph." Ollie scratched the stubble on his chin.

"Here it is," Millie stated, jabbing her finger at a black-bordered obituary. "I heard them talking about this one at the café—Lousie Windlesbacher."

Blood of the Lamb

"Who's that?" Ollie stared blankly.

"She lived next to my cousin Wilhelmina and her first husband, Kurt, when they had that farm by Yellow River."

"And you knew her?"

"Yah, we used to talk to her and her husband, what's his name." Millie scanned the death notice for a refresher. "Harold, no wait, he was the second one. Her first one, Jorgen. I would see them outside sometimes when we visited at Wilhelmina's house."

"And you want to go to her funeral? It sounds like you barely remember her."

"Oh I knew her alright. I was even in her house once. I went over to tell her that her dog's rope was all wound around some trees and he was barking his head off. She and Jorgen had a real tiny house. Smelled like mothballs."

"Is this funeral service more important than lunch? Couldn't we pay our respects after we get something to eat?"

"This is *where* we'll eat—Blood of the Lamb Baptist Church. 'Dinner will follow services, and burial later will be private.' It says the service started at one. It should just about be over now, and they'll be gettin' the food ready in the basement. Those ladies at Blood of the Lamb are casserole queens."

"Can't we eat somewhere else? I didn't know this lady at all, and we've missed the service completely by now."

"It's our duty to go to these things, Ollie. There aren't so many of us oldsters left around. I would feel bad if she didn't come to mine."

Millie folded the newspaper up and was rolling it into a tight tube to stuff back into the box when a face rose from nowhere to fill her window. Amos's hair stuck out in kinky antennas from any chink left open in the knitted scarf wound about his neck and head. What flesh remained exposed was

Snowplow Polka

cracked and weathered. An embroidered Green Bay Packers "G" could still be seen on the stocking cap that covered his forehead, but the green and gold had long ago surrendered to shades of brown. Even if you got close enough to have a real conversation with Amos, his pale green eyes never lost the frightened look that Ollie had often seen on trapped animals.

Today, a look of indignation and aggression quickly dropped into an expression of befuddlement. Obviously, the recluse did not recognize Ollie and Millie's new truck and had thought strangers were approaching his lair.

"It's you . . . You . . . you took my newspaper," Amos stammered, recognition mixed with accusation.

"We were just borrowing it," Millie explained. "A friend of ours passed away and we needed to check the obituary."

Ollie tried to lighten the mood further with some camaraderie. "I appreciate that you let us look at your paper, Amos. Could I plow out your drive for you? We'd do it for free."

"Never touch my path," the eccentric neighbor growled. "I wouldn't be able to see if intruders had approached. The perimeter would not be secure. And never take newspapers from my delivery box. I try to keep it stuffed so full there's no room for more. Then those idiots will stop delivering unwanted garbage here!"

Amos had taken a few steps back from the truck, and by the time he stopped, the shiny muzzle of a .30-06 rifle was clearly visible in his hand.

Millie appeared unfazed by Amos's aggressive stance. "Did you know Louise Windlesbacher from over by Yellow River? I'm sure your mom and dad did. You could ride with us over there to pay your respects if you'd like. I bet you'd see some of your friends, too. And they always have good food there."

Amos squinted and snarled: *"I hate, I despise your feasts, and*

Blood of the Lamb

I take no delight in your solemn assemblies. Even though you offer me your burnt offerings and grain offerings, I will not accept them; and the peace offerings of your fatted animals, I will not look upon them.'"

Ollie saw Millie's left hand move ever so slightly over the knob of the truck's stick shift, although her gaze never left their neighbor's haunted eyes. Ollie got the point and guided the transmission to reverse while lightly depressing the gas pedal. Millie, acting the charmer's part, never blinked to break the spell. As the snowplow crawled backwards, Amos moved into the center of the road to assume a guard's vigilant position. The rifle, though never lowered, at least was not pointed at them. It remained at an angle across the chest of the possessed sentry as he continued to admonish them: *"'Take away from me the noise of your songs; to the melody of your harps I will not listen. But let justice roll down like waters, and righteousness like an ever-flowing stream.'"*

❄

Blood of the Lamb Baptist Church was not exactly located in town. The Catholic and Lutheran churches had long ago staked out the best locations in Upper Mainz. The Baptists, considered latecomers to the area, had to build on a donated parcel in an adjoining settlement, named Clinton's Hollow, about three miles away. Though the church, built in the early thirties, was a nicely maintained white clapboard structure with an impressive steeple, it still suffered from comparisons to the brick and stone temples in town.

More recently, the Baptists had endured another slight. A young minister with unknown credentials had opened a storefront chapel in the former Ben Franklin space on Main Street, insisting on naming his new enterprise Blood of Our Savior.

Snowplow Polka

The Baptists felt that this upstart was deliberately watering down the term "blood" and causing confusion in the community. The mission in the rented space did at least spread the Good News, but it was exasperating to see how its rock-and-roll songs of praise and overly excited supplications to the Lord appealed to the younger families and eligible singles who would have contributed so greatly to the future of Blood of the Lamb.

When Ollie and Millie arrived at Clinton's Hollow, the situation there looked perfect. The church parking lot was still full, and the hearse was waiting sedately at the curb.

"This looks good. There's a lot more people here than I expected," Millie said.

"Yah, I thought you said nobody came to this church anymore."

"I guess nothing draws a crowd like a real good funeral. We should be able to slip right into the basement without anyone noticing."

The church had a side door that gave easy access to the secondary basement steps, which the workers most often used, but this approach would be too undignified. Besides, Millie reasoned, she really had known Louise, and they had a right to be there and share their condolences. Thoughts of the tuna noodle hot dish, with lots of crispy potato chips on top, reinforced her resolve as they climbed the front steps, passed through a set of glass doors and entered the foyer. They paused to listen in front of the sanctuary's closed wooden doors, each with one hand on a decorative iron handle. The organ reached a deep, sustained final note that would send the mourners off amid visions of heavenly gates thrown open in welcome. And indeed, the sanctuary doors did open, and the first mourners exited, facing the late arrivals.

Blood of the Lamb

In the churn of passing parishioners, some heading for the foyer stairs to the basement and others leaving the church, Millie and Ollie figured they would go unnoticed. Now they could be among the first to dash to the feast being served below.

Perfect, Millie thought. But she felt the tug of obligation and gestured to Ollie, leading him into the sanctuary. There she saw Louise laid out in a polished wood coffin that was simple but dignified.

Reverend Claire Crenshaw was consoling family members gathered near the altar. Eli Frost, the undertaker, was gathering and folding the blue satin coffin lining. While neatly tucking it in, he glanced up the aisle, catching sight of the tardy couple clad in snowmobile suits. Millie and Ollie were certain a shadow of disdain passed over his features before a saccharine smirk lifted the corners of his mouth to their usual position. Pausing in his duties, Eli drifted toward them, light and sinuous as the smoke from snuffed tapers, and bowed slightly in a show of respect for the bereaved.

"Mrs. Reinhart and Mr. . . . . Rolloff?" The undertaker hesitated on Ollie's name as if he were slightly unsure. "Were you friends of the deceased?"

His look of bewilderment did not hide the hint of inquisition. The problem of luncheon freeloaders was a current cause of complaint among the church ladies who labored to feed mourners at the small country parishes in the area. Eli had appointed himself watchdog, to maintain a sense of decorum should transgressors try to intrude upon a somber event.

Presenting a look of harried sadness, Millie answered, "Louise was a next-door neighbor to my cousin Wilhelmina when she lived by Yellow River. My husband, Virgil, and I would visit with her and Jorgen when we went to see my cousin."

Snowplow Polka

"Yes, Jorgen, he passed away in '78, or was it '79. Time does fly. Then I think it was around '82 that Harold and Louise were married and moved to Clinton's Hollow. Reverend Crenshaw often mentions to me what pillars of the church the Windlesbachers had become. I'm sure you remember when Louise and her family donated the Agnus Dei stained glass window next to the pulpit in memory of Harold's passing." Eli lifted his arm and pointed to the window that held a medallion depicting a reclining lamb.

"Agnes . . . Day?" Millie searched for meaning in the undertaker's lecture.

"Ah, yes, it's Latin for 'Lamb of God.'" Eli smiled benevolently. His encyclopedic memory wove a tapestry of family and church history that plainly put Millie on the outer fringes of Louise Windlesbacher's life. "I'll allow you to commune in private with the loved one before I close the coffin."

Millie watched as Eli floated off to join the family group from which soft sobs were emanating. Taking Ollie's hand, she shuffled at a respectful pace to the bier. Their snowmobile suits, with squeaky voluminous layers, gave them the appearance of astronauts trudging in slow motion on lunar soil. With heat building quickly inside the snow gear, Millie now realized that they were in an awkward position. If they kept the insulated outerwear on, they would swelter. If they took it off, they would be standing at the altar of Blood of the Lamb in dirty sweatpants and T-shirts.

The moment of silence that the two mourners shared began to seem uncomfortably long to Ollie. "Does she look the way you remember her?"

"Those eyeglasses don't look right to me."

"Maybe she got a new pair. When did you see her last?"

"Hmm . . . something's not the way I remember it. She

Blood of the Lamb

always had those pointy-up glasses, like cat's eyes. They were out of style even back then, but that was her look." Millie thought for a moment. "I bet undertakers lift the real glasses and just put costume spectacles on dead people. What would they be seeing in the dark anyway?"

"Time goes by so quickly," Ollie ruminated. "Fashions change."

"I guess I don't remember how she looked," Millie said softly, as tears began to well in her eyes.

"Are you alright, honey?" Ollie put an arm around her shoulder.

"It just seems like only yesterday that Virgil died," she sniffled. "I think maybe we should leave now."

"It's been a tough day," Ollie said. "We worked hard to do what's right, and we made a lot of people happy. Let's count our blessings. Bad things can happen at any time, but the Lord is always watching over us."

"That is such a lovely thought." The soft voice behind them interrupted their reflection and caught Millie and Ollie off guard. "You knew my grandmother? I'm Emily Gavin, Jonah's daughter."

"Oh, yes my dear. I'm Mildred Reinhart. Yes, I knew her years ago. But when I heard about her passing, I just wanted to visit with her one last time and pay my respects."

"That is so sweet," Emily said kindly. "You just never know how many people your loved ones touched until a time like this. I hope I'll be able to visit with you downstairs at the dinner. I'd love to hear about the memories you have of Granny."

"I wish we could stay longer, but my partner, Ollie, and I have to get back on the road. People are counting on us to plow them out. It's our business, ya know."

While they were saying their goodbyes and exiting to the

Snowplow Polka

foyer, Eli Frost unexpectedly reappeared between them and the outer glass doors. "I hope you're not leaving so soon," he said with a knowing look. "The ladies of the church have prepared a delicious dinner, and I'm sure the family would love to have you join them."

The sound of coffee cups rattling on saucers and the enticing scent of hot tuna casserole rose from the church basement.

"If only we could stay," Millie sighed. "But, duty calls."

"Excuse me, sorry I'm late." A portly woman with a serving tray jostled past them and headed for the stairs. Ollie caught only a glimpse of his favorite dessert being lofted away: cherry Jell-O with sliced strawberries and a dollop of Cool Whip on top.

❄

"'Hope you're not leaving so soon,'" Ollie grumbled as they walked out to the truck. "I don't think Eli Frost even knows who I am, but I imagine he's always on the lookout for new customers."

"Isn't Tuesday mac 'n' cheese day at the Cowbell Café?" Millie asked, giving Ollie a sly smile.

"You did the right thing in there, babe." He gave her hand a squeeze.

Memory Care

"Twenty-four pounds?" Rick Reinhart gasped, as he inspected the turkey his mother had displayed on the kitchen counter. The pink monster, with its pimply, feather-plucked flesh, bulged over the sides of Millie's largest roasting pan.

"Leftover Thanksgiving turkey makes a great freezer meal, Ricky," Millie said. "And besides, I'll bring some to your Aunt Rose in the nursing home, too."

"Aunt Rose is in the nursing home? I didn't know that."

"It's only been a little more than a week now. She had wanted so bad to be in her own place for the holidays, but your cousin Barb decided that enough was enough when she came to see her in October. Rose didn't even recognize her own daughter at first, and her feeble dog wasn't getting put out much, so the house was a mess. And Rose told Barb that she sleeps on her living room couch now."

"Why's that?" Rick asked as he tore open a bag of stuffing mix and dumped it into a pastel striped McCoy mixing bowl.

Millie stirred ground sausage in an electric skillet and said, "Rose told Barb that Gretel had moved into her bedroom."

"Gretel! Jeez, you mean that imaginary child your family always joked about and blamed for hiding things? Sounds like Aunt Rose is getting confused."

Tammy looked at her dad and said, "Isn't Gretel the fairy girl who takes my socks?"

"Yes, honey," Vicky chuckled as she chopped celery and onions to add to the sausage, "the same Gretel who hides your dad's reading glasses. You know that whenever something in Grandma Millie's house was missing when she was growing up, her family would always say, 'Gretel took it.'"

"Yeah, Tammy," Travis yelled from the living room, "she hides your socks under your bed."

Vicky turned toward the front room and replied, "And she's the one who took your homework, too. Right, Travis?"

"So what happened to her dog, to Timmy?" Rick asked.

"They took Timmy over to your uncle Richie's farm, but I think he has to live in the barn now—he's as confused as Rose."

"Poor thing," Vicky added. "That dog didn't have a tooth left to chew with."

"Mom, what did the dog eat?" asked Tammy.

"Canned food and steamed rice," Vicky said as she rinsed off the cutting board.

Millie finished cooking the meat and vegetables and poured them from the skillet into the mixing bowl. She then began jamming fistfuls of the hot concoction into the turkey's cavity.

Memory Care

"Grandma, you're using your hand to put that hot stuff in the bird?" Tammy asked with wide eyes.

"Sweetie, this is the only way to stuff a bird. You wanna give it a try?"

"No thank you . . . Maybe I'll watch the parade with Travis and Ollie."

Millie continued her conversation with Rick and Vicky, her arm in the turkey nearly to her elbow. "I was hoping we could all go over to Riceland and visit your Aunt Rose today while this here bird cooks. I know she'd love to see you all, and you just never know when it might be the last time."

A long groan emanated from the living room. Travis had looked up from his video game and was draped over the back of the sofa wearing a grimace. "Do I have to go to the nursing home, too?"

Vicky looked over at Rick and suggested an alternative. "Maybe Travis can stay here and watch the turkey while we go visit your aunt." Quietly, she added, "Tammy is too young to stay behind, though."

"We might as well go over to Riceland," Ollie agreed from his recliner. "This darn parade is no good anyway. The whole thing just stopped for this glittered-up kid to scream into a microphone."

"Ollie, she's famous—she's a star. I have her CD," said Travis.

"Where are the marching bands? What kind of balloon characters are those? Where's Donald Duck? Where's Goofy?" Ollie prodded the kids. "And that thing looks like a sponge."

Both the kids started giggling. "That's SpongeBob, Ollie!"

"Who the heck is SpongeBob?"

Ollie tossed the remote to Travis. He eased out of the recliner, went into the dining room, extracted a bag of nuts

Snowplow Polka

from a gift basket on the table, placed a pistachio between his teeth and opened it with a loud crack.

Millie turned from the stove and shook her finger, "Are you eatin' them pistachio nuts? I was gonna take that basket over to Rose's to cheer her up. And you're not supposed to be cracking nuts with your teeth."

"This basket was a gift to us from the Upper Mainz Electric Co-op. What would your sister do with fruit and nuts anyway?" asked Ollie.

"A gift, to *who*? Look at that label. It says 'Mrs. Mildred Reinhart.'"

"Can't we at least keep the pistachios? Rose is on a low-salt diet."

"Oh alright, ya cry baby. And I want those chocolate bonbons, too. Rose has sugar diabetes ya know."

Rick and Vicky watched as Millie went over to the table, dug a box of truffles from the cellophane-wrapped gift basket, re-taped the diminished parcel and returned to the kitchen.

Vicky cleared her throat. "You know, Mom, maybe those chocolate truffles aren't so good for you either. I thought the doctor told you to cut back on salt and sugar, too."

"Ollie and I burn off calories doin' our snowplow route. It's dangerous not to have energy snacks in the truck," Millie countered. "Vicky dear, I'm doin' my sister a favor by taking away these temptations and leaving her with the good stuff like apples and oranges."

Millie began stitching the stuffed bird using a long sewing needle threaded with white string. "This turkey will take five or six hours to roast. Travis, come in here so Grandma can show you something."

The lanky boy sauntered to the kitchen. "What's up, Grandma?"

Memory Care

Millie drew a long baster from her utensil drawer. She grabbed the red bulb and pointed the yellowed plastic syringe at her grandson. "You know what this is?" Travis looked incredulously at the tool and shook his head. "About every hour or so, ya open the oven and use this here to suck juice from the pan. Then ya squirt it on top of the turkey. That's basting. It keeps the bird moist, OK?"

Vicky watched this exchange, then said, "Travis, sweetie, are you getting what Grandma's saying? If you want to stay home, then you're in charge of seeing that this important job is done."

"Yeah, I get it. You squish the ball and you squirt the bird."

Millie gave her grandson a hug. "That's right, Travis. You're the man of the house now."

Then Vicky asked, "Shouldn't we preheat the oven before the turkey goes in?"

"I can't be waiting for that. We gotta get goin'." Millie heaved the enormous bird into her oven, set the temperature to 325 degrees and glanced at the kitchen clock. She then looked at Travis, compressed the baster bulb a few times to remind him, and placed it on the counter.

❄

Riceland was a pretty good-sized town of just over eight thousand, about 40 miles southwest of Upper Mainz. When the Park Avenue entered the zone of discount chain stores on the periphery of town, Millie gave directions from the backseat, "Don't ya see that sign Ricky? It's 45—slow down."

"That's right, this is a speed trap," Ollie affirmed. "Riceland balances its budget on Minnesota tourists that blow through town here every summer."

Snowplow Polka

Millie sat forward. "We can't have a ticket on our record ya know. We're commercial drivers now."

How did I get the privilege of driving this clunker, anyway? Rick wondered.

The highway became the main street of Riceland. In the center of town, a handsome mix of turn-of-the-century buildings still housed a variety of commercial enterprises.

"Dad, now the sign says 25," Tammy pointed out.

"OK, OK." Rick said with annoyance. He got ready to take the familiar turn from 1st Street to Euclid Avenue. "Is Aunt Rose at Golden Meadows, Mom?"

"There's no place else I know of," Millie answered. "I haven't been here since your uncle Martin passed away two years ago."

The impressive sandstone and granite building had once been the town's first private hospital, and it still featured wide front steps with a portico. A modern glass atrium now covered the main entry. The new addition had an enclosed lobby and a ramp for accessibility, so it was an improvement for most clients. The wide horseshoe drive remained unchanged though, and Rick dropped everyone off at the door before heading for the visitor's parking lot. Trying to shoehorn the unwieldy Park Avenue between the white lines in the lot would take some skill and faith.

As Rick walked up the drive, he saw his family coming back out the front door. "What happened?" he hollered through the frosty air.

When the group met him, Vicky answered, "They said your aunt isn't a resident here. They didn't know her or where she is."

"They said she might be over at Crown of Glory," Millie added. "Why didn't your cousin Barb tell me where her

Memory Care

mother was at? She knows this is where I'd go look. How'd I know they'd send her to some newfangled place?"

"Maybe we better call," Rick said. "Vicky, have you got your phone?"

"For goodness sake," Millie said, exasperated. "Rick, it's just over on Elm a few blocks past the tracks, and we don't even know the phone number."

"Vicky could get the information on Google."

Millie waved him off. "Oh, Google shmoogle."

❄

Crown of Glory was a modern single-story building with several wings. There wasn't any traffic in the front driveway, so Rick decided to leave the car by the curb and go in himself this time, to check at the front desk before parking and everyone having to get out.

"Schwartzberg . . . Schwartzberg. Rose, you said?" Rick had a sinking feeling already. The receptionist ran a thin finger down the computer monitor and searched the displayed list intently. It was obvious Aunt Rose wasn't here either, but the kind elderly lady, probably a volunteer who knew every resident, was intent on giving the impression that she truly believed him and would try her hardest to conjure up the lost relative from somewhere in the database.

Good thing that turkey takes several hours to cook, Rick thought as he saw his mother come barging in the door.

"I don't understand why I'm being sent all over Riceland just to find Rose." Agitated, Millie circled around behind the frail greeter's desk and stared at the pulsing screen. "Barb doesn't tell me anything. The lady at the other place said they hadn't seen her either. Just where are they keeping my sister?"

Snowplow Polka

Rick became aware that another conversation was going on behind him, and he looked with relief to see Vicky speaking softly into her phone. She met his eyes and held up one finger to show that she was almost there with the truth.

Vicky stepped forward and said, "She's at Riceland Rehabilitation Center, right behind the general hospital. I just talked to Cousin Barb. She said her mother's in room 313."

"What in the heck is she doin' there?" Millie asked with frustration.

"Sometimes seniors stay at the Center until there's an opening at a private facility," the meek receptionist suggested. "Our home here has a two-year waiting list."

"Well why didn't you say that to begin with?" blustered Millie as she shoved her family out the door. "Now we know where we're going!"

❋

The Riceland Rehabilitation Center was a brick and glass structure connected to the hospital by a second floor walkway. It was built where the parking lot had been. A new parking ramp was across the street, where the train depot had stood. The entry doors slipped open automatically with an efficient swoosh. The family entered the well-lit lobby of the rehabilitation center, where display boards advertised a facility with many patients who participated in a variety of creative activities. Taped to the tiled walls was a procession featuring colorful paper figures of pilgrim and Indian children, all carrying muskets, hunting a flock of turkeys. Upon closer inspection, the turkeys proved to be cut-out handprints, and within each print was a photo of one of the Center's patients.

Memory Care

"I remember when we made turkeys like that in first grade," Tammy reminisced.

"Hey, there's someone we know." They looked to see who Ollie had found. It turned out he was no longer studying the turkey hunt display, but pointing to a poster mounted on an easel that advertised an upcoming event.

"Well I'll be darned!" Millie said with amusement. On the poster was their good friend, the accordion-playing one-man-band Reggie VanArsdale. In a glossy promotional photo, Reggie was flashing a broad smile and wearing an Alpine hat with a braided band and a quail feather accent, and was playing an instrument inlaid with mother-of-pearl.

"It says Reggie's performing here today—in the Great Hall at one o'clock," Ollie added. "That's just precious! We'll bring Rose to hear him play."

The family took the elevator to the third floor, where a smiling nurse greeted them at an information desk.

"To visit Rose Schwartzberg?" Her pleasant voice held the lilt of a West African language. "Her daughter is here, and she told us you would be visiting. They're looking forward to seeing you. My, what a lovely large family!"

Millie breathed a sigh of relief. "Thank you very much. We've been running all over Riceland looking for my sister. I'm so glad we're here at last."

"Can you tell us where room 313 is?" Vicky asked.

"You go past the commons area and enter the hallway on your left. 313 is the third door on your right," the smiling nurse informed them.

In the open commons area an artificial fireplace added to the rustic log cabin décor. A wicker cornucopia filled with dried gourds rested on an oak leaf garland that decorated the mantle. Many of the unit's patients and visitors were gathered in this comfortable living room. Some people were working on jigsaw puzzles, playing cards or watching a large-screen TV with the volume turned low.

Rose's room was rather small, and Barb got up from one of only two chairs to welcome them. "Well look who's here! Look Mom, Millie's here to see you. And Ollie, too, and the kids. What a surprise!"

Aunt Rose looked delighted, but when she embraced her sister she said, "Oh Millie, you shouldn't have come all this way to see me. I'm only going to be here for a few days. I don't know why the doctor thinks I need a rest—all I did was rest at home anyway."

The other family members pressed into the room with a penguin-like sideways shuffle so everyone would fit.

"Oh, who else is here?" Rose looked to see the beaming clan gathered around her bed. "Ricky and Vicky, I don't believe it! And is that little Tammy? How did you get so tall?"

Everyone breathed a hidden sigh of relief at Aunt Rose's lucidity. Even if Barb had prepped Rose for their arrival, she still sounded genuinely aware of each person and overjoyed to have a room full of visitors. Rose was also nicely dressed in rich chocolate-colored velour pants and a matching jacket that boasted an embroidered holly pattern around the neckline.

"She's having a very good day," Barb whispered under her breath to her cousin Rick.

Ollie held out the gift basket wrapped in red cellophane. "We brought you a present, Rose."

"Oh you shouldn't have! Look at the size of that basket. Is there room for it on the counter by the other one?"

Along the window ledge, next to a neat row of cards and

a bouquet of purple mums, was an identical basket to the one they had brought.

"The electric co-op delivered that one to Mom's house, so I thought I'd bring it here," Barb explained. "I figured the staff could help her eat it."

"Maybe two is a bit much," Millie concluded when she realized that her re-gifting ploy had been exposed.

"Mom does love those chocolate truffles. I'm sure we could find a way to use everything if you really don't need it yourself, Auntie."

"I'm sure the staff is well enough fed, Barb," Millie huffed, then crammed the crinkling basket into her son's hands. "You take this back to the Cities, Rick, and let the kids have a special treat from Grandma."

"Will we even get the pistachios and chocolates, Grandma?" Tammy blurted.

A change of subject was needed, and Ollie was quick on the draw. "We saw a poster in the lobby that Reggie the Polka Man is playing here in half an hour. Do you think you'd like to go there and listen, Rose? Maybe cut a rug with me?"

"Reggie . . . the Polka Man? Cut a rug, Ollie?" Rose looked bewildered.

Barb swiftly took control. "Mom, there's going to be a musician playing in the Great Hall today. We should let Fatima at the information desk know that you're going with us to hear him. I think we'd all enjoy it."

"Polka dancing? That sounds like fun . . ." Rose smiled. But then, with consternation, she added, "Oh, but I try not to leave the room you know. Anytime I'm not watching, Gretel might come out."

Rose looked abashed. Barb muttered to Vicky, "I told her not to talk about Gretel."

Snowplow Polka

"Gretel?" Millie asked. "The imaginary little girl we always blamed when things went missing at home? Rose dear, don't worry about that, we're here now." Millie leaned closer and patted her sister's hand lovingly.

Rose reached out and drew Millie's head nearer. Frantic whispering ensued. "She followed me here. I don't know how. I thought she'd stay at my house."

"I'm sure Gretel isn't here. How would someone hide in this cramped room?" Millie said.

Rose urgently pointed toward her mattress several times. "I think she's under the bed. I hope she's asleep."

The entire family had gathered around to hear this secret confession. Now they exchanged glances and stepped back from the bed. Tammy was preparing to squat and check under the bed frame when she saw Barb frowning and shaking her head back and forth vigorously.

"I think it would be a lot of fun to go hear Reggie play." Barb bubbled with over-enthusiastic encouragement. "You never get out and talk to the other nice people, Mom. If this Gretel is around here it would be a perfect time for her to leave and visit someone else."

A ripple of nervous laughter moved through the group as they started to shuffle out of the narrow room.

❄

Music with a rousing tempo was pulsing from the Great Hall and reverberating into the corridor as the family approached. Reggie had managed to contort "Angels We Have Heard on High" into a yodeling invitation to dance. His voice was hardly the angelic choir that the carol promised, but his accordion trills were soaring to wondrous heights. Even patients using

Memory Care

walkers were stepping about on the dance floor while several surprisingly spry couples displayed some very graceful turns. Staff members also twirled wheelchair-bound patients to the happy rhythm. When "Gloria in Excelsis Deo" came to a raucous last stanza, the crowd sang along and clapped in time. Reggie had his sleigh bell pantaloons on, and he shook them in a joyous ringing finale.

"And with that angelic medley, we have launched the holiday season here at Riceland Rehabilitation Center!" Reggie proclaimed. Looking out from a small carpeted platform, he saw his friends enter the hall. "The music will continue in five minutes, ladies and gentlemen. I imagine you might need a short break after that heavenly carol—I know I do."

The one-man band wove his way through the slowly departing dancers to Ollie and Millie and their family. "I didn't expect to see you folks here! You're not turning yourself in are you, Ollie?" the musician teased.

"No, 'I ain't goin' to the home, no way!'" Ollie sang back.

"Reggie, I want you to meet my sister, Rose Schwartzberg," Millie said. "She's staying here for a little while, and she's been dying to hear some of that good old-time music."

The entertainer made a deep bow and doffed his dark green Alpine hat. In her honor he nimbly ran through a chorus of "The Last Rose of Summer" on his accordion. Aunt Rose blushed and flipped her hand in a tsk-tsk gesture at the flattering charmer.

"If it's some old-time music we need, then that's what we shall have." Reggie took Rose's hand and held it out to Rick. "For a dance partner I recommend your handsome nephew, Sir Richard. Whatever you do, don't let that Ollie, with his two left feet, steal you away. He'll crush your toes with his elephant-walk polka."

Snowplow Polka

"Oh don't listen to that silver-tongued devil, Rose," Ollie said, pretending to be hurt by having his talents belittled. "I was voted best senior male dancer at last year's VFW Jamboree."

Back on stage Reggie knew that he couldn't stray too far from the Christmas carol theme of the concert, so he went directly into the ever-reliable "I Remember Christmas Polka." The residents in the crowd carefully got to their feet again, and the floor was soon full. Rose grinned from ear to ear. Rick adjusted his dancing pace to her condition, though he didn't hesitate to send her into a few good spins.

"I'm so glad we came to hear your friend, Aunt Millie," Barb enthused. "This will show Mom how many great things there are to do here with the other seniors. She's hoping she'll only be here a short time. A social worker is helping us evaluate her needs."

"Change is always difficult, Barb, and I know your mom misses her house," Millie replied. "But there's nothing like a polka to get you back in a happy state of mind."

Tammy looked up at her mother and asked, "Can I go back to Aunt Rose's room and get my book bag? I left it on the window ledge."

"Gee, I'm not sure. Can you find your way by yourself?" Vicky asked.

"I remember how to get there, room 313. It will only take me a minute—don't worry about me, Mom."

❄

"All by yourself this time?" Fatima looked at Tammy who had returned to the third-floor information desk.

"Is it OK if I go and get my book bag in Aunt Rose's room?"

Memory Care

"Alright my little lemur, but go directly to your auntie's room, children can't be in the hallway here."

❄

Tammy opened the door. The room was dark. Feeling the wall just inside, she flipped a switch, but instead of the overhead fluorescents, a light in the bathroom came on. Curious, she went to inspect this private space. In a glass by the sink, a pair of dentures floated in a liquid that released occasional bubbles.

Great Aunt Rose wears dentures? She walked closer to get a better look at this specimen. The air in the room had a cloying, powdery bouquet that Tammy didn't recognize.

Great Aunt Rose always has rose perfume in her bathroom, just like her name, Mom always says. She unscrewed the lid of a powder box and sniffed its contents—it didn't smell like a rose.

There was also an appliance of unknown function hanging from the shower curtain rod, a floppy plastic bag with hoses dangling from it. She had just stepped over to investigate this when a small movement near the door caught her attention. Ever so slightly the knob was turning. Her heart began to pound.

The door opened with the agonizing slowness of a horror movie sequence, revealing an elderly lady who hunched forward and had a crooked grin. Tammy quickly realized she had entered the wrong room.

"I'm sorry, I thought this was my Great Aunt Rose's room. I'm in the wrong place."

"No my dear, you're in the right place." The woman extended a trembling hand as if to pat Tammy gently on the head.

"My name's Tammy. I'm here with my parents to visit Rose

Snowplow Polka

Schwartzberg. She's staying in 313. I think she's your next-door neighbor." Tammy pressed herself against the bathroom door frame and began to wiggle past the fawning woman's grasp.

The lady eyed the girl as if she were a hummingbird about to flit off. "Would you like a tasty chocolate my dear? There's a lovely box on my dresser, and I really shouldn't eat them all myself."

To Tammy, this sounded suspiciously like the witch's invitation to Snow White. Still, it would be awfully rude to just bolt out the door, and that large gold and green foiled candy box did look alluring. "Maybe I could try just one. Then I have to go to my Aunt Rose's room. They'll be wondering where I am."

Tammy lifted the box lid. A faint aroma of syrupy sweetness and cocoa was still present, but the age of the contents was alarmingly obvious. Only a few spaces were vacant, where crenellated paper cups now stayed as place markers. Nearly all the remaining treats had been cracked or pinched open at some time. Their chocolate shells were in pieces and the soft centers had oozed out and crystallized. An overall white growth covered the entire arrangement with a dusty film.

"I always have to make sure there are no nuts inside before I eat a piece. With my teeth, I can never eat nuts again." The woman's explanation didn't ease Tammy's growing concern. "And coconut, oh that's too stringy. You probably remember, I never did like lemon flavor either."

"I guess I really shouldn't spoil my appetite. When we get home, Grandma's got a whole Thanksgiving dinner ready for us."

The fragile woman put a shaking hand on the girl's arm and pleaded, "Stay awhile longer, Tammy."

But Tammy backed quickly toward the door, managing to get "I'm sorry I disturbed you" out before she ran to the hallway. Looking back, she saw that the elderly lady was not about to end her pursuit. With candy box in hand, she began to move toward the door of her room, apparently thinking that the irresistible chocolates might still lure the lost child back in.

The hallway was empty, and Fatima wasn't at the desk. Tammy thought about dashing to the Great Hall, where she knew everyone had gone for the dance.

Then, seeing number 313, she instead rushed into Aunt Rose's room and scrunched between the chairs and the bed.

Keep going . . . keep going. Tammy's brain willed the woman to keep moving along the corridor, but instead a quivering shadow outlined by the hallway lights, paused in the doorway to room 313.

"Tammy, are you here? Did you forget your lemon cream?"

Tammy slid quietly to the floor and saw beneath the bed frame that the pursuing figure had entered the room.

The hunched woman was now beside the bed, preparing to look behind the chairs. Tammy continued a worm-like slither beneath the bed, burrowing so deeply that she was certain she couldn't be seen. Then there was silence. Just when she felt she could not hold her breath another second, the elderly woman began to hobble back toward the door. A moment later cries of "Tammy! . . . Tammy! . . . Tammy?" echoed in the outer hall.

"Mrs. Whitesmann, can I help you?" Fatima's gentle voice came from the corridor. "I see you're carrying that candy box again. Why don't we just take that back to your room."

Next, Tammy heard her grandma's voice—her dad's and Ollie's, too. In an instant the overhead lights came on and the room was full of people. Tammy struggled to get out, but the bed frame's constricted space made it hard to move.

Snowplow Polka

As her head popped from under the fringe of the coverlet, a loud gasp resounded in Great Aunt Rose's room. The relieved girl looked up to see a collection of astonished faces.

Laughing, then, Rick said, "Gretel, it's you!"

Cold Turkey

"I do believe your sister hasn't had so much excitement in years," Ollie professed as he looked over his shoulder at Millie, who was sitting next to Tammy and Vicky in the backseat of the Buick. "And she sure cut a rug with me on 'Grandma Got Run Over by a Reindeer'!"

Millie smiled. "You're right—I bet she hasn't polkaed in ages. Rose used to be one of the best dancers in town. It was hard to compete when she was on the floor."

"I danced with her today, too, and she still knows all the steps," added Rick. "And did you see the way she looked when Tammy crawled out from under her bed?"

Snowplow Polka

"Dad! That wasn't funny, and it wasn't my fault. I was hiding from that lady who wanted to give me candy."

Vicky put an arm around her daughter and drew her close. "It was just an accident. Don't listen to your dad—he thinks everything is funny."

❄

By the time the Park Avenue made its final descent into the lake home's driveway, Millie could hardly contain her excitement. "I just can't wait to smell that juicy bird cooking!"

"There's nothing like a home-cooked Thanksgiving meal with all the trimmings," Rick said. "Your stuffing is the greatest, Mom."

Tammy chimed in, "And don't forget the pumpkin pie I helped make—my favorite!"

The car had barely come to rest in the garage before Millie's door swung open and she trotted into the house. The rest of the family emerged slowly, stretching after the forty-five minute drive, and then filed in behind the mother hen. Ollie got the well-traveled gift basket out of the trunk and closed the garage door.

Millie hurried through the hall toward the kitchen, knowing just what to expect. But not even a whiff of roasted turkey was in the air. Baffled, she spun around, went into the living room, looked over at the blaring TV and then down at the couch. "Travis! Are you asleep on the job?" She started shaking the groggy kid. "What's wrong with the turkey? Where's the smell? Where's the smell!"

"Smell? What smell?" Travis mumbled, blinking at his grandmother. "I don't smell anything."

Cold Turkey

"I think that's the point, son," Rick said with foreboding as the rest of the group followed him into the living room.

Vicky rushed to assist her mother-in-law. Together they bent over the stove. Millie dramatically flung open the oven door to assess the turkey's condition. Rick and Ollie hung back—a front-row seat wasn't necessary for following this drama. The bird lay as fleshy and uncooked as it had when Millie put it in the oven before they left to visit Rose.

"Travis! Your assignment was to be basting this! Didn't you see that there was a problem? Why didn't you call me?" Vicky implored.

"I was just getting ready to baste it, but it didn't smell like it was cooking yet. I fell asleep for awhile, I guess."

Millie and Vicky both stood cautiously and began to scrutinize the accident scene, trying to reconstruct the tragedy.

"What is the temperature set at?" Vickie asked.

"Three twenty-five," replied Millie.

"Dial set to bake?"

"Check."

"Did you press the On button?"

"Yup, the red light's on. We did everything right." Millie spun around. "You men get over here and figure out what's busted."

Rick and Ollie moved forward to evaluate the appliance.

"Sure enough, the On/Off switch is red, so there's electricity," Rick observed.

"And the inside light came on when they opened the door," Ollie concurred.

"Electricity, yes, but gas?" Rick removed a panel near the floor and used a flashlight to explore this bottom chamber. "I don't see a pilot light, and I don't smell gas. It must have gone out."

Snowplow Polka

Ollie knelt beside Rick. "Here's a lighter."

"Doesn't this stove have an electronic pilot light?" Rick asked Ollie. "Jeez Louise—lighting a pilot manually seems like some ritual from another era."

He flicked the disposable lighter. "No gas, nothing happened. I'm going outside to check the propane tank in the backyard."

After a few minutes, Rick was back in the hallway, stomping his boots and brushing snow off his pant legs. "What the heck happened to the tank, the large one?"

"I told the co-op to bring me a smaller tank," Millie answered. "Ollie and I never use much propane anymore. It's just the two of us, and besides, we have to save money any way we can."

"You weren't saving money by ordering a smaller tank; the tanks belong to the co-op. Anyway, you only pay for as much propane as you use. Right now, the gauge on your little tank reads zero. That means the gas space heater in the basement must be out too. Thank God you've also got electric baseboard heat here."

"I can't believe the delivery man from the co-op wouldn't come out and inspect that for me. I never ran out of gas during the winter before. I try not to use just the electric heat cuz it's so expensive."

"That big space heater downstairs helps to keep the whole house warm. If it goes out, then yeah, the electric baseboard heat is on all the time. You needed the full-size propane tank to fuel that. It doesn't matter how many people are in the house—it still has to be heated. Just look at that puny thing you ordered! It looks like a scuba tank!"

The whole family gathered together and looked out the dining room window at Rick's footprints leading from the

Cold Turkey

garage backdoor through the snow out to the downsized container.

"Look at the size of that thing!" Travis exclaimed, "It's huge!" Across the snow covered backyard a solitary figure leading a horse interrupted the family's viewing of the propane tank.

"Is that Uncle Richie's horse?" Tammy asked. "Titus?"

"Sure is," Millie said. "Richie lets Amos borrow Titus when he needs stuff hauled—and tools, too. And we always let him cross our property to get to the lake."

Amos Nedahammer led the Belgian draft horse, which was dragging a sledge that had an ice shack balanced on it. Amos did not acknowledge them; he just looked ahead, one hand behind him, tugging on the horse's lead. Titus looked as noncommittal and placid as his guide, moving his shaggy hooves through the snow without complaint and blowing white clouds of breath from his nostrils.

"What a cool fishing shack!" Travis said with awe. "That thing gets better every year. Look at what he does with beer kegs, man!"

"His ice shack has turned into a miniature version of his house," Rick said, amused. "That's what you call armored siding. And look at that satellite dish on the roof—and a bullhorn, too. That's a new addition."

"The ice can't be thick enough to hold that!" Vicky said with concern.

"Don't worry—he's just going to drop it on the shore now," Ollie explained. "But he'll be the first to get his shack on the lake as soon as the ice will support it."

Millie nodded and said, "And you can bet he'll park it right over that underwater gravel ledge just off Vanderweir's Point. Plenty of people in town would like to claim that spot, but

Snowplow Polka

Amos always gets there first. That's the same place his dad always fished."

"Yah, I know that spot," Rick said. "The fish are always biting there."

"That's right," concluded Ollie. "OK kids, the show's over and we're hungry. I'll call the co-op about the propane in the morning, but in the meantime, I know just the place for a great Thanksgiving dinner."

❄

Vicky was naive enough to wonder if the Winneboujou Casino would even be open on a national holiday like Thanksgiving. But her doubts dissipated long before the Buick even neared Upper Mainz. A pair of rotating searchlights crisscrossed the low cloud bank hypnotically, drawing in one and all with the promise of reward. Although they were still a mile and a half from the casino, taillights began to flash red on the highway, and a long backup had begun.

By the time the illuminated facade of tall poles arranged to resemble teepee ribs came into view, the traffic was at a lurching crawl.

"Holy cow! Did everyone's oven break?" Rick grumbled as they inched forward. "You would think the sign said 'Free Beer.'"

Instead, the gaudy marquee proclaimed, "Welcome Pilgrims! TKSgiving Buffet All WKend!"

"Now you'll be glad I brought my handicapped permit along!" Ollie trumpeted.

"That's right," Millie added with an I-told-you-so harrumph. "Rick, you think the lines are bad out here? Wait till you see the buffet line. Then you'll be happy I grabbed my walker."

Cold Turkey

"Is that the walker you inherited when Uncle Martin passed away?" Rick asked.

"Yah, that's right," his mother affirmed. "That fancy red one he had. It's always one of the top-rated models in the *AARP Bulletin*. It's got handbrakes, a nice wire basket and a built-in seat."

"Didn't they give you another one last winter when you slipped on the ice and sprained your ankle?" Vicky asked.

"Right. Medicare will give you a basic walker if the doctor prescribes it, but luckily I had Marty's Cadillac model to help me get around."

"We use it at Costco," Ollie added. "Your mom needs it sometimes—that store is so dang enormous."

"Oh Ollie, don't talk about that in front of the kids," Mille protested. "And your handicapped permit isn't just window decoration either. You're the one who had two heart attacks and has trouble going five dances without getting short of breath."

"But won't people question the fact that last week you drove a snowplow?" Rick inquired. "And today you're so disabled you need a walker?"

"That's the beauty of this thing, Ricky. I've actually done something that could aggravate my foot. Snow removal is the perfect excuse."

❄

When at last they'd made it into the parking lot, it turned out that all the handicap-accessible spaces were taken. Ollie cursed the vehicles he recognized whose drivers he believed were no more disabled than he was.

Millie conceded to pay for valet parking, but it turned out

Snowplow Polka

all the valet spots were also occupied. A brusque attendant with a lighted wand then pointed the way to an outlying lot from which they could be shuttled back. Millie was forced to drag Uncle Martin's walker up the shuttle bus steps while an impatient crowd watched her slow charade. Phase one of their disability act was not going so well.

Still, as Millie reached the main entrance she got excited when all the adults received free raffle tickets for prizes that would be distributed throughout the evening. The greeter took one look at the children—who were not normally allowed into the casino—and directed their party to a corridor designated by red velvet ropes toward the dining facilities. While management seemed to have accepted that today's patrons were more interested in cheap food than cheap slots, those waiting in line had a clear view beyond the velvet ropes of the activity on the gambling floor.

Travis gawked and said, "I feel like I'm in a video game! See that huge flat-screen TV? It looks like the robo-chick is dealing cards." Rick snagged Travis's arm before he could duck under the rope for a closer look.

Vicky turned to Rick with a murmured complaint. "I wish the kids didn't have to see what's going on in the casino."

"Mom and Ollie really love this place, Vicky. I know they eat here a lot more often than they're willing to admit. Let's just try to enjoy our dinner."

The express line for disabled patrons and their families was nearly as long as the regular queue for the dinner buffet. Apparently, a large number of customers had at least one family member who was disabled. Millie, leaning on her walker, fielded continual greetings from friends and relatives who were also waiting in line.

"Millie, is that foot acting up again?"

Cold Turkey

"Oh, I know you two are so busy you don't have time to cook."

"So nice to be with the loved ones on holidays, dontcha think?"

All the marvelous scents of Thanksgiving were wafting from the chafing dishes in the serving area: roasted turkey's intoxicating aroma was complemented by sage high notes and underscored by a yeasty baked biscuit foundation, all crowned by pumpkin pie spice.

Millie inhaled deeply. "Ahh, those wonderful smells. It's funny that I had to come to the casino for this. We always made a special meal together at home, but it looks like everyone else in town celebrates here. Doesn't that smell great?" She looked over at her granddaughter, who was pinching her nose. "You don't like it?"

"It's the cigarette smoke, Grandma. It stinks. It's bad for you."

"Adults do a lot of things out there in the casino that kids don't do. The good news, sweetie, is that there's no smoking in the dining room," consoled Millie.

❄

In the Reinhart party of six, Ollie was the least capable of waiting patiently in line. He paced back and forth along the queue like a scout checking for weak spots. Every few minutes he dashed into the dining room, looking for patrons preparing to depart, under the guise of offering greetings to friends and polka dancing pals.

While Ollie worked the crowd in the dining room, Millie talked with Rick. "Remember when they built this place? Everyone in town was so excited—it put Upper Mainz on the

Snowplow Polka

map. There never used to be anything to do out here, and now people come to our town in buses."

"Yup, this was quite the swanky joint when it opened. They haven't updated it much, though."

"What do you mean, why would they update it? Don't you love this hunting lodge look? And those stars twinkling like the Milky Way on the ceiling—it's just like up north."

"I was gonna mention," Rick countered, "that it seems like the Milky Way is hidden by a cloud of smoke."

Vicky, Millie and the kids all looked at the casino ceiling, and it was true, there wasn't a star in sight.

"I don't see how you can say this place hasn't been updated, Dad," Travis said with a look of awe. "Check out that cool *Lord of the Rings* game over there—it's got wizards and a dragon and everything. And how about that *Family Guy* machine? I love that show!"

Vicky furrowed her brow. "*Family Guy*—I told you not to watch that."

"That's not the only thing our kids shouldn't be seeing. How about the *Walking Dead* slots?" Rick pointed over the velvet rope at a nearby row of video zombies.

Just then, a voice rang across the casino through loudspeakers. "Ladies and gentlemen, it's time for our first hourly winning raffle numbers. Get out your tickets. Remember, one random drawing tonight will be for the grand prize of five hundred dollars. Here's our first number: 3, 7, 4, 9, 8, 9."

There was a scream near the bar, and the announcer said, "We have a winner!"

Tammy jumped around with excitement. "Mom, Dad, Grandma—keep your tickets out, they're going to call another number! We could win!"

Millie handed her ticket to Tammy. "You be my good-luck

Cold Turkey

charm, sweetie. Those numbers are too small for Grandma to read."

The announcer came back on and read off two more sets of numbers.

"No winners in that bunch for the Reinhart family," Rick concluded.

"And now for our final number this hour," said the amplified voice. "2, 0, 1, 3, 8, 5."

A squeal rang out from Tammy, and she tugged on Millie's arm. "Grandma, Grandma, we won! We got the number!"

Rick squinted and examined the fine print. Sure enough, the numbers matched. "Do you want me to go and get the prize, Mom?"

"No way! Tammy and I will take care of this. It's our prize."

The family and all the people standing in the buffet line watched Millie slowly roll her way to the host stand. The hostess placed a bulging plastic bag in the basket of Millie's walker.

On her return, elated friends gave Millie high-fives and pats on the back. Tammy glowed proudly beside her grandmother.

"What's in your basket, Mom? Rick asked. "A bag of money?"

"I won a frozen turkey!" Millie exclaimed.

A chattering gaggle of women immediately in front of Millie and her offspring—three elderly ladies accompanied by their middle-aged daughters—turned to them, and one exclaimed, "You won a turkey! How lucky is that!"

Ollie came rushing back to see what all the commotion was about. "What happened? Rumor has it you won a prize."

"Grandma won a turkey," Travis replied, with a wide grin.

"Aw, that's precious, babe." Ollie bent over and gave Millie a kiss. "This is our lucky day at the casino."

Snowplow Polka

Millie lifted out the prized turkey and looked at it with jubilation. "Rick, take this beauty out to the car. Ollie's got a cooler in the trunk."

On his way toward the door, Rick whispered to Vicky, "If I'm not back in time, load up your dinner plate for two."

One of the mothers in the party ahead of the Reinharts said to Ollie, "I sure hope that good luck rubs off on us. Those nickel slots we were playing seemed pretty tight tonight."

Her daughter joined in the conversation. "My mom and her girlfriends just love playing the nickel slots."

Another of the younger women quipped, "Every time I call my mother, she's not home."

The third batted her eyelashes as she spoke to Ollie. "We hear she's having an affair with a one-armed-bandit."

The three mothers giggled and blushed. With hands aflutter, they pooh-poohed their daughter's comments. One said, "We're just having fun, girls. Don't get your panties in a bunch. It's only nickels."

Millie took Ollie aside and whispered in his ear, "I think I know a way we can move to the front of the line. Those chicks ahead of us are dying to get back in the action. If they heard the nickels were paying out, I bet they'd break ranks and head for the casino floor. Get my drift?"

Above the normal volume of conversation, Ollie stated, "I just get so nervous standing in this line. I heard there's been some winning hands at the Texas Hold'em tables. I gotta go see what's happening."

"He's off again," Millie clucked loudly, as Ollie ambled away.

Tammy took Vicky's hand and asked, "Why did that lady ahead of us say her mother knew a one-armed-bandit?"

Cold Turkey

"That's just casino talk," Vicky said, pointing toward one of the classic slot machines. "See that game over there with pictures of fruit and a long handle attached to its side? That handle is the arm. You pull on it, and if all the cherries line up in a row, money will fall into the tray."

"But why is it a bandit, Mom?"

"Because it takes a whole lot more of your money than it gives back, and that's robbery." Vicky sniffed.

Ollie returned a few minutes later and gave an especially audible report. "You wouldn't believe the action over at the nickel slot pit. One lucky lady hit the jackpot, and then the winning kind of spread like wildfire. Those darn machines are dumping nickels like diamonds from the sky."

All the buffet line patrons in the vicinity seemed energized by this tall tale of good fortune. Some began to fidget anxiously, while others exchanged personal yarns of past gold rushes they'd been party to. A few fell for Ollie's bluff, forgetting about dinner and making a mad dash for the nickel arena at the far end of the building.

The elderly ladies ahead of the Reinhart clan had caught the spark. "Girls, girls, did you hear that? Things are starting to open up. I knew as soon as this lucky lady won a prize, we were gonna be next. Let's hit those slots and get in on the winnings."

The younger women tried to reason with their agitated mothers. "Don't you want to eat? It's Thanksgiving! We've been waiting in this line a long time, and we're next!" But the deck was stacked against them.

"What's one more hour? We're here to have fun. Dinner is served twenty-four hours a day anyway." The three older ladies bolted for the casino floor and the put-upon daughters were swept along behind them.

Snowplow Polka

Shortly after that, the dining room hostess emerged with a notepad. She surveyed the diminished line with a perplexed look. She glanced back at her list and then called out, "Reinhart? Party of six?"

Village on Ice

A lumbering Pontiac Bonneville slowed to a crawl at the intersection of County Road K and 2¼ Streets.

"I think 2¼ goes toward the lake here, but I don't think we've gone far enough yet to be near the turnoff for that fancy chalet," said Hank. "Maybe we should stay on K and keep going north a ways more."

"What did that biker dude at the Double Eagle Bar say again?" his buddy asked.

"He thought you might take 2¼, but it could be another road that connects with that.

Snowplow Polka

"Why the hell isn't there just a road that goes around the friggin' lake?" Jedidiah swore nervously. "I feel like a rat running through a maze out here."

"These all used to be private roads to farms that bordered Little Butternut. But the farmers sold their lake lots for cabins and this whole mess happened," Hank explained.

"We could see that big-ass chalet from the cemetery across the lake, so we gotta be gettin' near it."

"Let's try this 2¼. We can't be sitting here long or people will notice us."

"Damn! Couldn't you have stolen a car with a better heater?" Jedidiah whined as he blew into his hands and rubbed them together.

"I guess robbers can't be choosers, Jed," chuckled Hank, as he eased the car forward. "We were lucky to find this tank. Good thing I looked in the garage over at that cabin on Tamarack Lake."

"I don't know what's so great about this gas hog."

"Nobody looks at a clunker like this. They're all over the place out here. And nobody will go to that cabin until spring, so it won't be reported missing for months. Wisconsin plates, too."

"I'm keeping a look out for something with a good heater, though," Jed said, getting in one last complaint.

The two thieves reached another intersection. Ahead on 2¼ there was a dead-end sign and the road dropped away to a long wooded peninsula that jutted out into the lake. On their right, a newer gravel road, 14½, continued north and disappeared around a bend.

"What do you think?" Hank asked.

"Let's finish checking out this dead end first, if that's not right we'll come back here to 14½."

Village on Ice

Hank drove the Bonneville down the road. They passed an A-frame house from the fifties, then a rundown turquoise-and-white mobile home that had been put on blocks and converted to a seasonal cabin.

"Pretty slim pickings," Jedidiah snorted as he appraised the dwellings.

"Wait," said Hank as they approached the last driveway. "This isn't the chalet we saw from across the lake, but it's a good-sized house, not like those seasonal shacks we just passed."

"And do you see what I see?" Jedidiah asked.

"Uh-huh," Hank replied.

There in the driveway was the distinctive F-250 snowplow that had roused them from their sleep at the rest stop back in November.

The robbers' eyes met and flashed mischievously. Then Jed said, "So this is where that nosy geezer lives. I betcha that baby's got a pretty good heater in it."

Hank held his hand out to silence him. "I saw something."

"At that house?"

"No, off to your side—in the woods."

"A deer?"

"No, something else. I think we're being watched."

"You're hallucinating."

"I got a bad feeling. You know when I get that feeling it's time to move on."

As the Bonneville reversed and turned around, Jed looked back and hissed, "You and your bad feelings. I'm not forgettin' 'bout this place."

"Yup, it's on our shopping list."

Snowplow Polka

Three snowmobiles roared through the ditch along the fields of Nels Gustafson's farm. Racing up the sides, the daredevils nearly put their front skis over the crest of the embankment before turning back into the trough and then zooming up the other side.

Then the trio revved up, shot out from the depression and, with open throttles, made a final sprint across the fields. Savage whoops poured from the helmeted hellions as they cut a path through corn stubble that split off in a choppy wake. There were plenty of low spots where a snowmobile could glide smoothly onto Little Butternut Lake, but what would be the thrill in that? Instead, each snowmobile charged onto a ridge, went airborne for a few careless seconds and then dropped jarringly onto the ice sheet before its tread regained traction, sending it out across the frozen lake, toward a cluster of ice fishing shacks.

This ice shanty village was known to all on the lake as a hangout for young rowdies. The constant stream of loud music and boisterous shouts kept serious fishermen, seeking solitude on the ice, far away. The village's only close neighbor was Amos Nedahammer in his aluminum monolith.

As the snowmobilers drove to their gathering spot, they made certain to circle the hermit's shack several times first. After screaming like banshees and cutting almost close enough to nick the metal siding, they congratulated themselves on their bravery, but were disappointed to get no reaction.

Their friends, hearing the commotion of the arrival, piled out of the shacks. When at last the engines had died, chests had been thumped, and beer cans popped open, everyone got to the business at hand: displaying their catch of the day.

Village on Ice

The group of fishermen watched as two acne-shot teenagers lifted three small fish from their bucket. "You call that a catch?" someone scoffed.

"Two perch and a pike!" needled another guy.

"We caught other ones, but threw them back," one of the crestfallen teens replied.

"I got two crappies," a swaggering fisherman added.

Joining the weigh-in, another angler said, "I got a twelve-inch walleye."

The fish didn't look like twelve inches, but nobody wanted to spoil this small victory by getting out a tape measure.

"I musta had some monster muskie," a bearded fisherman bragged. "Frickin' pole bent right in half. I could hardly hang on to the thing. Lost my frickin' lure when the line snapped." The stocky boaster swayed on his feet as he spun this fable, the stench of marijuana smoke seeping from his beard and the creases of his dirty flame orange coveralls.

There was no need to say much more—the group's pathetic haul spoke for itself.

"When I got those two crappies, I thought we were all gonna start haulin' 'em in, then it just kinda . . . died."

"We're not close enough to the underwater gravel ledge to get good crappies here."

"That damn Amos is parked right over the best spot on this whole side of the lake."

"I bet he's got a stringer full of crappies already."

"Hardly seems fair that the same guy gets all the best fish in the lake every year."

They glared toward Amos's full-metal abode.

"I just know he's watching us right now. That sucker has spy holes cut all over his weird shack."

Snowplow Polka

Incited by this derogatory bile, one of the new arrivals reached over and scooped some slush from beside an open hole in the ice, packing it with his deer-hide choppers into an icy ball. He lobbed it, and the missile sailed in a perfect arc that ended with a loud clang on the roof of Amos's fishing house.

"Way to go dude! Great shot!" the bearded guy cheered.

Quiet ensued, while the ruffians paused to see if there would be any results from their instigation. Then a disembodied voice emanated from the bullhorn on top of the shimmering shelter and echoed across the bay.

"Hear this word, you cows of Bashan, who oppress the poor, who crush the needy. The Lord God has sworn by his holiness that, behold, the days are coming upon you, when they shall take you away with hooks, even the last of you with fishhooks. And you shall go out through the breaches, every one straight ahead; and you shall be cast out into Harmon."

As Amos's words died away, an eerie calm descended. Then the fishing mob, possessed of a single mind, began hollering and cursing. They all ran to gather the iciest snow and pound it into an arsenal of fist-size balls. Projectiles dappled the air, homing in on Amos's shack. With the merciless shotgun spread, enough missiles hit their mark to make the metal-clad outpost reverberate in a shuddering drone.

When this onslaught brought no retaliation, the hotheads stoked their ire to new heights with blasphemous cries. Several of them fired up their snowmobiles, twisting accelerator grips to full throttle and made the short run to the loner's shack, smacking its aluminum sides with fists and spare gear. The bragging angler even grabbed his twelve-inch walleye by its tail and bludgeoned Amos's shack until a pink mess of scale-flecked meat and guts splattered across the side.

Village on Ice

Suddenly the just anger of the Lord poured forth again from the bullhorn, its metallic vibrato ringing above the howling snowmobilers.

"They hate him who reproves in the gate, and they abhor him who speaks the truth. Therefore because you trample on the poor and exact taxes of grain from him, for I know how many are your transgressions and how great are your sins—you who afflict the righteous, who take a bribe, and turn aside the needy in the gate. Therefore he who is prudent will keep silent in such a time, for it is an evil time."

"Damn your bunch of Bible bullshit, Amos!"

"I'm the one who's gonna trample something, you loony bastard! The door to your house!"

"Ya better drag this eyesore shack off this ledge and let someone else catch a damn fish around here!"

Riotous jabs from the inflamed crowd grew to a crescendo while the denunciations from the bullhorn rose in volume with quotations that now left reality far behind. *"Therefore thus says the Lord: 'Your wife shall be a prostitute in the city, and your sons and your daughters shall fall by the sword, and your land shall be divided up with a measuring line; you yourself shall die in an unclean land.'"*

"God almighty, what a nut job!"

Beer cans, garbage and the remainder of the day's catch rained upon the besieged fortress.

"I've got some bungee cords here. Let's hook 'em to this crappy shack and drag it to the other side of the frickin' lake!"

"Yeah! Gimme one of those bungees."

Amid the heckling jeers and bombastic Old Testament prophesies, one fisherman walked right over to the shack and started searching for anchor points.

All at once, the door of the armored shed burst open and a double-barreled shotgun stuck out. The harassed victim

Snowplow Polka

pointed his weapon toward the heavens, but there was no doubting the seriousness of his intent. A deafening gunshot rocked the bay.

The hooligans froze in open-mouthed alarm. Then, while the report was still echoing off distant shores, a mad dash to the snowmobiles took place. Slipping on slush and fish guts, the terrorized oafs made an inglorious retreat, bringing their machines to life with panicked speed. The sleds scurried away in disjointed zigzags, leaving the scene of the crime far behind.

❄

The next morning, Sheriff Trost stopped at the Cowbell Café to fortify himself before dealing with the incident. Helmuth got the feeling that the eatery had been buzzing with gossip before he arrived because the conversation dropped to a low mumble when he opened the door. At the back of the café a TV mounted high in a corner showed the local news with the sound turned off.

"I'll have the corned beef hash and short stack this morning, Cora," the sheriff called out to the waitress as he took a seat at the counter facing the kitchen.

Only Vern Nelson and Sam Grittner were at the front table where the local business owners usually sat. The morning crew knew that the sheriff had some unpleasant business to attend to.

At his makeshift office, Rupert Everson appeared to be too immersed in his typing to even acknowledge the new arrival. *Probably writing my obituary*, Helmuth thought. *No Pastor Skagen or Father Dougherty today? What if I need last rights?*

"Oh! Here comes the weather report." Cora grabbed the TV remote and turned on the volume.

Village on Ice

On the TV screen, an earnest young man dressed in a suit and tie stood before a map of the upper Midwest, gesturing toward a collection of curves, letters and arrows. ". . . And we can expect blizzard-like conditions all the way from northern Iowa, through south and central Minnesota and into northwest Wisconsin, as a low pressure system coming from the south rides the ridge of cold Canadian air that has settled into our region."

"Where's El Niño when you need him?" Sam muttered.

"He's been bumped off by an Alberta Clipper," Vern snickered back.

The weatherman continued: ". . . The stage is set for the two colliding fronts to produce six to twelve inches of snow over the next several days. There could be areas where pockets of instability in the atmosphere or microbursts of lake-effect snow could combine to generate even greater accumulations."

Sam acted perplexed, "What the hell does that mean?"

"It means you should close the drugstore and come help me sell shovels and snowblowers," Vern replied with a grin.

Cora shot them a quick look of friendly annoyance. "Can we just listen to the weather report without the commentary for a second, you two?"

". . . Look for temperatures in the single digits in our neck of the woods, with windchill readings falling into the dangerous twenty below category by the weekend."

Another lovely day in Upper Mainz, mused Sheriff Trost. He looked at his watch absent-mindedly. *How long until I retire?*

After the weather forecast, Cora muted the TV again, and the only sounds to be heard were the clinking of silverware on ceramic plates. Another minute passed, then Vern cleared his throat and addressed Helmuth. "Looks like you got your job cut out for you today, eh, Sheriff?"

Snowplow Polka

Rupert stopped typing and looked over to hear if there would be any breaking news.

"Nedahammer crossed the line yesterday," Sam added. "Discharging a firearm at some ice fishermen—that's a serious offense, right?"

Cora slapped a bar towel on the counter to get Vern and Sam's attention. "From what I heard, your 'ice fishermen' were that obnoxious bunch that usually hangs out at the Double Eagle Bar." She topped off Helmuth's coffee before continuing. "Those characters threatened Amos. Why do they always have to park their fishing shacks next door to him, anyway?"

"Humph," was the only response from Helmuth.

"Seems to me a person has a right to put his ice shack anywhere he pleases on that lake," Sam huffed. "There's no property lines out there."

"That may be true," Cora said, "but there are a lot of other people fishing that lake, and they never have a run-in with their neighbors."

"The politics of how these ice fishing villages get established would make an interesting news story on its own," Rupert reflected. "Families practically will their fishing spots to the next generation."

Vern threw his arms up in frustration. "In this area, not only do they will their fishing spots, but they pass along those overbuilt plywood ice houses, too. I got top-of-the-line portable ice fishing shelters at my hardware store that are lightweight, easy to move, and don't freeze into the ice. But do people around here buy them? Hell no!"

Helmuth turned around on his stool and chuckled. "Those plywood junkers really are a pain. Every spring we have those dang sheds frozen onto the lake and you have to threaten and ticket people to get them off the ice before it thaws. It costs

Village on Ice

them money, and it wastes my time." Then he turned back toward the counter and said, "Two insulated cups of coffee to go, Cora, and two maple glazed donuts with chocolate sprinkles in one of your little white bags."

The café regulars watched through the front window as the sheriff trudged to his cruiser.

Sam took the toothpick from his mouth and said, "There he goes to Ice Station Zebra."

"Why does Amos cover his shacks with aluminum anyway?" Vern asked.

"Something to do with aliens I always heard," Cora replied.

"But is he trying to repel them or attract them? That's the question," Sam mused.

❄

Amos was awakened by an intense ray of early-morning sunlight coming through a peephole in the door of his ice shack. He had tried to stay alert all night, worried that the snowmobile mob would return. *Morning? I must have dozed off.*

On the door, through which the shaft of light pierced, hung a large picture of his ultimate hero, Our Lord Jesus Christ. In this famous sacred heart portrayal, Jesus raises his right hand in a two-fingered sign of blessing and draws back his cloak with his left hand for the big reveal. There, upon his chest, a starburst surrounds his bleeding heart, which is engulfed in flames. Within the fiery heart is a crown of thorns. In the center of this ring, Amos had drilled a small hole and inserted a spyglass. Through that hole in the Son of God's heart, Amos could see anyone who approached the door of his sanctuary.

Amos got up to open a shutter on a side window, letting more daylight into the small interior. He stretched his stiff

Snowplow Polka

muscles and surveyed the ice fishing village nearby. "All clear, so far," he reported to himself with a yawn.

The increasing light revealed pictures of Amos's other favorite martyred saints mounted to the front wall of the shack, surrounding the door. These were enlarged reproductions of holy cards that Amos had used as bookmarks in his childhood Bible. Each of these holy men had made the ultimate sacrifice and was now glorified in a scene that depicted their untimely death.

Amos looked over at the picture of Saint Sebastian, who was stripped naked, bound to a tree and shot through with arrows. *That was his moment of glory.* Sebastian's eyes were always raised pitifully to the Lord above, praying that God would soon cradle him in his arms. *He never lost his faith.*

Ah, Lawrence. He must be the best of them all. Amos shook his head and smiled. *You gotta love a guy who asks his torturers to flip him over when he's being grilled alive over open flames.*

At last, he looked to Saint Canutus, all decked out in priestly garb, his arms spread wide and a spear projecting right out of his chest. *That's it, thank you very much, Lord! What do you want, man? I'm a priest, I'm in church, I'm praying, and all of a sudden, a big old javelin flies through the window and kills me. Thank you so very much for that.*

Amos felt that his martyr heroes could provide some group support; but in the end, he knew, everyone had to stand alone.

With his meditation on saintly lives concluded, Amos bent forward to check the view outside through the peephole in Christ's heart. Off in the distance, a dark figure was approaching across the white sheet of ice. Amos growled, "Here come da judge!"

❄

Village on Ice

Sheriff Trost had decided to wait until broad daylight before going to deal with Amos Nedahammer. To advance with the rising sun at his back might give the best strategic advantage, but why antagonize the loner by resorting to military tactics? Truth be told, he half-wished the hermit had unloaded a volley of buckshot into the backsides of the town's delinquents. Even the distorted yarns that these bullies had spun at the Double Eagle Bar hadn't sounded like much more than self-defense on Amos's part. But investigating any disturbance, even at a fish house, could quickly flare into a dangerous confrontation, and obviously the suspect was armed.

Helmuth thought he would get to the lake by taking the trail that ran along the northern boundary of Nels Gustafson's farm. This steeply descending route, seldom used in winter, was nothing more than a cow path between upper and lower pastures. Still, it was the shortest way to the cluster of ice fishing shacks that was his destination. Helmuth was determined not to raise any fears of a sneak attack, so he decided to approach Amos's shack head on.

In one hand Helmuth carried the cardboard tray with two Styrofoam cups of coffee. In his other hand he held the paper bag of donuts, leaving his holstered gun securely strapped and in plain sight. *Oops—jeez it's slippery. No wonder Nels keeps the cows off this slope in winter,* the sheriff thought, juggling the peace offerings and trying to keep his balance.

Not another soul was on the lake that morning. Presumably, the neighbors were peeking through curtains, waiting for the showdown. Some raucous crows, picking at dead fish and trash on the ice, provided the only soundtrack for the encounter.

Amos's metal shed glimmered in the winter sunlight. When the sheriff was about fifty yards away, the bullhorn crackled to life and an apocalyptic prophecy began.

Snowplow Polka

"'They do not know how to do right,' declares the Lord, 'those who store up violence and robbery in their strongholds.' Therefore thus says the Lord God: 'An adversary shall surround the land and bring down your defenses from you, and your strongholds shall be plundered.'"

"Amos!" yelled Helmuth. "Hey, for God's sake, cut the preaching and open the darn door. You can see I got my hands full."

There was a lull, then the sound of a latch being released. The door opened slowly, with a metallic groan. Helmuth moved toward the dimly lit cavern and stepped inside.

"I brought coffee," he said. "Better drink it while it's still warm."

"Looks like ya brought something else, too. What smells like maple?"

Without waiting for an invitation, Amos took the waxed-paper bag and dug out a donut. Sitting down, he chomped into it, leaving glaze stuck to his beard and mustache.

"Is the other one for you, or are they both for me?"

"Help yourself. No breakfast, eh?" Helmuth was pleased that Amos had accepted the coffee and donuts; it looked like a good sign.

The fishing shack was about the size of a double outhouse. There was enough room for two men in bulky gear to sit together on the bench, but not much more. Two holes cut in the floor led to two holes cut in the ice. Helmuth stepped cautiously to avoid the hole in the floor at his feet as he surveyed the tight space. A dented red Coleman cooler, a giant-sized thermos, the heater, and a propane lamp rounded out the furnishings. The double-barreled shotgun sat propped in the corner next to Amos.

Village on Ice

For an ice fishing shack, the walls were very carefully decorated. The collage of religious iconography on the front wall made for a colorful, if gruesome, presentation. On the back wall, a display of photos, mainly black and white, was arranged with the same obsessive neatness. Rows of young men in military uniform had been carefully placed in a somber grid.

This must have been Amos' army unit from the Vietnam War, Helmuth figured. *Those poor kids.* Some had allowed a slight smile for Mom, and others looked like fawns caught in headlights, but most clenched their jaws in determined, battle-ready seriousness.

"A lot of the fish houses I visit have pictures of naked women all over the inside," Helmuth said.

"A clean mind draws the right line," was Amos's reply.

The sheriff contemplated this cipher, and then took a seat next to Amos on the bench.

"What the hell happened out here yesterday?"

The recluse didn't answer for quite a while. He slowly sipped the last dregs of his coffee. He then brushed off his beard with one of the napkins Cora had stuck in the bag. The sheriff was sure his suspect didn't feel that he needed to justify his actions; nonetheless, it would be nice to have a statement to put in the report.

"Little bastards tried to scare me off my spot. Came and threw ice balls and dead fish at my house. Said they were gonna drag it away."

"And you discharged a firearm within the village limits?" asked the sheriff.

During another long pause, Amos neatly refolded the napkin and stuck it under his red cooler. "I made a mistake. I sank to the level of my tormentors. Vengeance is reserved for the Lord."

Snowplow Polka

Helmuth paused, and then turned to look at the army photographs again. "What does 'Ne Desit Virtus' mean?" he asked, referring to the Latin inscription in the center of the portraits.

"Let valor not fail."

The sheriff squinted at some small printing done long ago with red marker next to an X on a map of Vietnam. "What was Operation Apache Snow?"

"It was an order for martyrs to march to the top of a hill."

"That must have been an important hill."

"No."

"The guys with black circles around their pictures—they were killed?"

"In action. The ones with a red circle have died since they got back here. The rest are still in their shells."

"In their shells?"

"The shells they were given to walk around in when they got back home."

The two men sat without speaking while Amos adjusted the slack on his ice fishing rod.

Helmuth rubbed his clean shaven chin, then said, "You know, Amos, a person with your experience might be a lot of help to me out here. I don't know what you've heard, but there's been some trouble around the lakes. A couple of cabins have been burglarized, and last month someone robbed a year-round home and stole guns and ammo. This is a serious problem." The sheriff paused then prodded some more. "Have you seen anything suspicious?"

Crunching his empty coffee cup and tossing it into a bucket, Amos reached over, inspected his fishing tip-up in the second hole, and said, "I did see something the other day. A

Village on Ice

car drove real slow past my place, and then it stopped at the top of Reinharts' driveway. I didn't like what I saw."

"What color?" Helmuth quizzed.

"Uh . . . dark green."

"What make?"

"Something big—GM, I think. I wasn't that close."

"Could you see who was driving?"

"I was back in the woods, by my place. All I saw was two guys, maybe."

"That's it?"

"Yup."

Sheriff Trost stood and zipped his jacket all the way up for the walk back. "You know why I had to come out here today, right?"

Amos gave him no response, no eye contact.

"Let's put this incident to rest and concentrate on the more important problems going on around here," Helmuth advised. "I appreciate the fact that you could tell me what you saw by the Reinharts' place. If you see anything else unusual, it would help if you let me know. By the way, they say it's gonna start snowing at sundown and not stop for two days. You should probably head home soon."

"I know."

Helmuth opened the door and stepped out into the blinding white world. To the southwest, clouds were starting to darken the horizon. The sheriff looked back and nodded to the hermit in his cloister as he closed the door. His walk across the frozen lake began as a quiet time for contemplation. But before he could reach the shoreline, the armistice was broken by a haunting last quote from the bullhorn.

"Surely I will never forget any of their deeds. Shall not the land tremble on this account, and everyone mourn who dwells in it. 'And

Snowplow Polka

on that day,' declares the Lord God, 'I will make the sun go down at noon, and darken the earth in broad daylight. I will turn your feasts into mourning and all your songs into lamentation; I will bring sackcloth on every waist and baldness on every head; I will make it like the mourning for an only son and the end of it like a bitter day.'"

When the sheriff had made the slippery climb back to where he'd parked, he saw Nels Gustafson come out of his barn and hurry over.

"I heard that gunshot yesterday, Sheriff. Are you gonna have to arrest the guy?"

"I don't think so, Nels. Amos thought it might have been a wolf pack out there, but it turned out to be just some loose dogs he scared off. I might have to deputize him if he keeps doin' my work for me." As he headed over to his squad car, Helmuth tossed the last of the cold coffee from his cup, making a short brown stain across the snow.

Dust Off Your Lederhosen

"I ain't wearin' no leather shorts!" Ollie declared defiantly. He watched Millie continue to dig through a pile of antique clothes that were kept in a cedar chest at the foot of the bed.

"Here they are. All they need is a spruce-up." Millie began to buff a pair of dark green lederhosen with a suede brush. She knew there wasn't much need to answer Ollie's complaint—this argument had become a yearly holiday ritual.

"I feel funny getting into Virgil's old pants. That was part of his German family background, not mine. No self-respecting Norwegian wants to be seen in Bavarian beer hall shorts."

With a sugary voice and the kind of sweet smile a patient

Snowplow Polka

mother uses on her stubborn child, Millie responded, "We go over this every year, Ollie. The Christmas polka dance is a time for everyone to remember the past and celebrate traditions. You know how all the younger kids look forward to seeing these classic costumes this one special day of the year."

She figured that Ollie just wanted to be able to assure his male chums that he had put up a good fight and none of this had been his idea.

Millie held the lederhosen up against Ollie to admire them, "These will still fit you perfectly! I don't think you've gained an ounce this year." She lovingly studied the details of the garment. "I remember when these leather trim pieces were nearly red and the stitching around the itty-bitty flowers used to be so white. But what I really like about these pants is that deer cameo on the chest strap."

"Uh huh," Ollie conceded. "That leaping stag is a beauty alright—carved from a real antler. And . . . are you going to wear the matching Oktoberfest getup?"

"It's a dirndl, Ollie—yes. The same one I wore last year for the Christmas dance." Millie walked over to the closet dedicated to their dancing outfits. As she slid open the door, it revealed a tightly packed history of polka fashions. She flipped through a collection of floral patterns, layers of lace, and acres of petticoats. When she reached a group of her favorite polka-dot dresses, she knew the dirndl would be next. The antique dress was protectively sealed in its own garment bag, and, like the lederhosen, was only worn for the holidays.

"Is it really necessary to get all this clothing out of storage now?" Ollie asked. "The dance isn't until Sunday."

Millie unzipped the garment bag and removed her outfit. "I'm taking all these things to my basement sewing room. I remember this dress needs some hem work. I always like to air

Dust Off Your Lederhosen

out those suede pants, too. And you need to polish your shoes. Besides, Ollie, didn't you hear the weather report this morning? It's gonna snow for two days and not stop till Saturday night. You know what that means."

"I don't even think they're going to hold the dance on Sunday. I bet they cancel it cuz-a this blizzard."

"'They'! Who the hell is 'they'? You and me and Richie and Eunice and Cora worked all those days to decorate the trees and put up the crepe paper and hang the crystal ball. We're the ones to say if the dance is canceled, and it ain't canceled!"

"Oh? And who's gonna be there? What about the Sandberg girls? They can't hardly drive even in dry weather. And Fred and Adelaide way out by Lost Lake? Even Reggie—his driveway is so darn long he'll never get it cleared in time."

Millie tossed the heavy lederhosen onto the bed and stood upright, all five feet and six inches, like a rooster in mid-crow. With hands on hips and one eyebrow cocked as a bushy exclamation point, she laid down the unquestionable law of the land: "That damn Christmas dance is on for Sunday night, even if you and I have to drive from here to Lost Lake and plow out every single one of those dancers. You hear me, Ollie? It's on!"

❄

The last flakes drifted past the floodlight mounted above the garage doors at about three-thirty Sunday morning. The storm was over, and the howling wind that came behind it seemed to have blown itself out. Ollie looked through the window in the front door at a world transformed. Against the dark backdrop of night, the glaring light revealed a high-peaked meringue of snow that blanketed everything, leaving only a mounded suggestion of what had once been familiar forms.

Snowplow Polka

Beautiful. There was no other word to describe that scene. Not even rabbit tracks had disturbed the pristine view. *If only I could just stand here and contemplate it,* Ollie thought, *not fight it, plow it, curse it, or dig, dig, dig, through it.*

"Have you fallen asleep standing up?" Millie asked as she came up behind him. "Just look at all that snow! Ya wouldn't know we'd plowed out the driveway twice already yesterday. I hope you have enough gas in that truck."

Inside the garage, the two partners mounted the bench seat of the mighty F-250, dragged the seat belts over their cumbersome snowsuits and turned the radio dial to the Eau Claire "Northwoods News." Ollie pressed the button on the garage door opener. As they watched the paneled portal creak upward, a new two-foot drift came into view just outside the garage door. Their headlights bounced off this compacted snow, which then collapsed into the garage.

"So, what are ya waitin' for?" Millie prodded. "Let's tackle this baby!"

"I was just thinking," Ollie said. "When I was looking out the front door at what this storm left behind, I thought, every time it snows the earth looks so renewed, so unspoiled. And it reminds me of how beautiful this country must have been before people arrived and put their mark on it."

"My, aren't you the poetic one today, Mr. Rolloff."

❄

Ollie wouldn't go so far as to say "Practice makes perfect," but the snowfalls of November and early December had made him a pretty experienced plow driver. Being familiar with the twists, turns and small idiosyncrasies of the route had made him much faster, and more competent, too. Of course, if he ever

Dust Off Your Lederhosen

did need a reminder, Millie was right there beside him reciting a litany of every close call and wrong turn they had encountered that winter. The near-formless landscape that had once been so intimidating was becoming familiar territory to the pair. Ollie had to smile when he thought about how critical he had been of his predecessor, Swany Swanson. In the full grip of winter, with landmarks and property lines obscured by heaps of snow, it was all you could do sometimes to just keep the truck on the road. *If the occasional mailbox or fence post gets smashed, so what?—file your complaint with the township. Let's see you try this.*

"Yippee-ki-yay! Ride 'em, cowboy!" Ollie whooped, as the tough Ford took on the highest drifts and threw monster plumes of white off into the frozen fields. "You're gonna have no excuse to miss church this morning, ya poor sinners. I think Pastor Skagen should split the collection with us for plowing the path for his flock!"

"You betcha!" Millie enthusiastically seconded. "At this rate, we'll have plenty of time to get ready for the dance. Let's drive this herd to Omaha!"

❆

It was a sad truth that the plow driver's driveway was the last one finished. Ollie was so tired after getting out of bed early, sitting there on a stiff seat all day and gripping the wheel till his fingers locked, that he felt like just hauling himself into the house and collapsing. But that wasn't the way he had been raised by his Norwegian mother. With rhythmic sweeping scrapes, the driveway got cleaned as neatly as a barber would shave a face.

When all the plowing was done, the rumbling F-250 sat in

Snowplow Polka

the center of a perfectly manicured swath of gravel. The Reinhart homestead looked like a wilderness outpost waiting to be photographed for a holiday card.

From the truck's high seats, Millie and Ollie dropped carefully to the ground. With legs wobbly from sitting tensely in the cab all morning, they shuffled to the house.

As soon as they got in, the blinking light of the answering machine on the end table next to the recliner in the living room signaled distress. The drivers were used to looking over at the recorder whenever they got back from their route—it seemed like someone always had at least one complaint. Millie jabbed the play button.

"You have eight new messages," the mechanical voice declared, then it began to deliver the first one. "Ya. Ahh, Ollie? Millie? Ya, this is Walter, over at the community center. Well, ah, you know, I had to plow the lot at the high school today, and ah, . . ."

"Land sakes, spit it out!" Millie scoffed as she punched the stop button, cutting off Walter Bing in mid-drone. "So, he didn't do his job and get the community center lot plowed out. What a nimrod!"

She tapped the play button on again. "Ollie, Millie, it's me, Reggie. I got halfway done with the drive when my snowblower choked and froze up. There's no way I'm putting my hands near that thing to clean it out—I gotta play accordion. Not only that, my car won't start. I don't know if you two will get out this far, but I can't think of any other way I could get to the dance through this snow. Call me back."

"So the lot ain't plowed and the musician can't make it. Some holiday dance!" Ollie said with distain. "OK, let's hear the next one."

"Yoo-hoo, you two lovebirds. It's Beulah and Bertha Sand-

Dust Off Your Lederhosen

berg. You just don't know how much we were looking forward to the dance tonight, but oh golly, the county plow left a mountain of snow at the end of our drive, and we don't know when our grandson will be by to help shovel us out. Looks like we can't join you this year, but we'll be thinking about you kids, you betcha. Toodle-oo, you dears."

Millie pressed the pause button and looked at Ollie.

Ollie was already looking at Millie. Reading her expression he said, "I can see that I'm not going to be watching the Packers game this afternoon."

"That's right. Here's the plan: First, drive into town, get gas at the Rheinview Co-op, and go over to the community center and get that lot plowed. Try to get the snow cleared by the side door, too. While you're gone, I'll listen to all these messages and figure a way to dig these dancers out of their houses. And if you see anyone in town, be sure to tell them that the dance is still on. Got it? Go!"

※

Upon his return from town, where the community center lot had been dotted with cars abandoned mid-blizzard, Ollie staggered up the steps from the garage into the house and dragged himself through the hallway, past the kitchen to the living room. Before he even got his coat off, he heard Millie dictating instructions.

"It is now four-thirteen, the dance starts at six, and we have time to do this as long as we follow my plan and don't dilly-dally."

Ollie made his way over to the open doors of Virgil's former office. He hoped desperately for some time to catch his breath, and looked jealously at the half-empty beer bottle on

Snowplow Polka

the desk in front of Millie. "It took forever to get that community center plowed out real good and make sure all the entrances from the street were clear, too. Plus, I saw Helmuth handing out tickets left and right. He'll let folks in town know that the dance is still on."

"I know all that. I've been on the phone in here nonstop since you left, calming all these nervous Nellies and letting them know we'll be right over to rescue them."

All dolled up in her dance costume, Millie looked like a sugar plum fairy in the big leather office chair. The petticoats under her dirndl gave the impression that she was floating above the seat. The desk had been turned into a command center. Scribbled-upon papers fanned out around her on the surface and spilled onto the floor. A county map marked with an orange highlighter was spread open on her lap. A clipboard, the office telephone, an open tin of sardines and the beer were all within arm's reach.

"Strap those lederhosen on, mein Herr. We'll go out to Reggie's first—he's the farthest away and we need him the most. I have the route all mapped out."

Millie got to her feet, attached the itinerary and map to the clipboard, tucked it under her arm, grabbed her purse, and then with her free hand balanced a sardine on a saltine cracker. Pointing the way with this tidbit, she said, "I'll take care of this mess later. Time's a-wastin'."

"Can't I get something to eat first?" The quaking in Ollie's voice was no act—he was bushed.

"Oh my poor hard-working driver," Millie said sympathetically, suddenly realizing that there might be another world beyond her cyclone of activity. She dropped everything but the cracker onto the desk, put her arm around the haggard

Dust Off Your Lederhosen

man and directed him to sit in the office chair. "Of course there's time to eat. You've been working all day. Some of those yahoos in town can do something, too, by golly. You just stay here while I get ya a snack."

Millie left the room and headed for the kitchen. Ollie heard the refrigerator door slam shut. She was back in a flash with a block of Limburger cheese and links of leftover gritzwurst on a wooden cutting board, and a tall glass of cranberry juice spiked with a spoonful of honey. "I ate almost all the sardines while I sat here talking—there's only one left," she reported.

The silver fish, slathered in mustard—which had been sitting on a cracker for the last ten minutes—she now held out as a reward. Millie put the morsel to her lover's lips. When he bit on the head end, she quickly leaned over and bit the tail so that their mouths met in the middle for a fishy kiss.

"Ahh . . . fishes and kisses and cheese," Ollie said with renewed vigor. "Everything a Wisconsinite needs."

❄

A break in the wall of tall black spruce trees, and Reggie's mailbox, floating bravely on a sea of white waves, were the only indications that there might be a road leading off into the woods. Ollie accelerated to a fast pace on County Road OO, then cut the wheel sharply and rammed into the hardened berm that the county plow had left at the end of the driveway. If he hadn't guessed correctly about the location of the road, the Ford would have gone right into the ditch. But his aim was true, and even though the plow truck bucked and groaned at this harsh command, it cut cleanly to the roadbed and lifted only a light hail of gravel with the snow plume. Soon

Snowplow Polka

the remote homestead was in sight, and Reggie himself was visible through the large picture window in his living room, jumping about and playing his instrument with zeal.

"Looks like Reggie found the time to practice and is raring to go," Millie observed.

When his driveway was cleared, Reggie leaned out the door and extended a steaming mug of coffee as an invitation.

Millie grabbed the microphone and shouted over the bullhorn, "Forget the coffee, just grab your squeeze-box and get out here, ya hoppin' kraut muncher."

"Can you imagine living in a dinky house like that with a man who plays accordion and dances around like he's cuckoo?" she asked Ollie while they waited. "No wonder poor Hedwig passed away so young, gone in her prime."

"Yah, but he must have entertained her to the end," Ollie chuckled.

The musician stuffed two accordions, a binder of sheet music, and a bag of assorted percussion instruments into the crew cab and then hauled himself in next to them. Reggie was grinning from ear to ear. No sooner had he settled in than he opened a case, lifted out an accordion and began running his fingers over the keyboard.

"Oh no ya don't!" Ollie objected. "This cab's hardly got enough room for the three of us, and if you start pumping that thing I won't be able to hear myself think."

"Oh hang on just a minute. I can't let this song get away!" Reggie enthused. "Wait till you hear what I just concocted!"

Their passenger was not about to have his creativity stifled. He beamed with the glow of an inspired artist.

"When I heard you were coming to rescue me in your snowplow, I just got hit with such a great idea that I grabbed my accordion and let 'er rip."

Dust Off Your Lederhosen

Millie elbowed Ollie and said, "There's no stopping an idea whose time has come."

Reggie tried to adjust for the confined space, but the opening notes still made for a jarring racket in the truck's cab. Then he began to sing.

> Let's all do the snowplow polka!
> Push, push, shove, shove, beep, beep!
> Let's all do the snowplow polka!
> Push, push, shove, shove, beep, beep!

The first line of the chorus soared like a yodel. Then when he sang, "Push, push, shove shove, beep beep" these three replies chugged and paused with the backbeat of a puffing steam engine.

"The 'Snowplow Polka'?" Millie beamed.

"I'm making it up as we go!" Reggie chortled. "Millie, grab your clipboard and write what you hear me say. I think if I see the words later, I'll remember the tune."

> Oh it's snowin' like the devil,
> a blizzard so they say.
> But we can call on Ollie,
> He'll blow it all away.

When Reggie repeated the chorus, Ollie and Millie joined in on the catchy replies. The musician continued adding more lines. He followed each new stanza with the snowplow polka refrain, and before long they were all bouncing in their seats and singing.

Snowplow Polka

Oh da storm it was so monstrous,
the dance was gonna close.
"No way," says my friend Ollie,
"They'd miss my lederhose'."

Oh da peoples was so frightened,
they closed der doors to hide.
But not that good old Ollie—
grabbed his plow 'n' took a ride.

Now the farmers and their daughters
was a-scared to go outside.
But not that good old Ollie—
he's got Millie by his side.

As the merry trio sang the final verse, Ollie slammed on the brakes. They all jerked forward, and Reggie's accordion rammed into the back of Millie's seat.

"What the heck are you stopping for?" she demanded.

"We just passed County P. We gotta go there to get the Sandberg girls."

"By God, you're right. I got so busy singing, I forgot to look at my list."

Ollie drove back about eighty yards and turned onto P. It had been plowed earlier, but open fields allowed the winds to redistribute a lot of loose snow and pack it back onto the sides of the road.

"Looks like I'll do the county a favor and keep P plowed out, at least to Sandbergs' farm." Ollie dropped the blade and scraped snow off the blacktop as they rode.

"I got a great idea!" Millie exclaimed. "When we get to Beulah and Bertha's place, we'll all start singing again, I'll turn

Dust Off Your Lederhosen

on the microphone, and we'll broadcast our song over the bullhorn!"

❄

By the time they reached Lost Lake, the plow truck had dug out four other couples—their vehicles now formed a caravan following the Pied Piper.

"Lost Lake really lives up to its name," Reggie joked. "Fred and Adelaide are at the intersection of nothing and nowhere."

Ollie agreed. "Some people really like their privacy."

"But they sure do love to dance when they come into town," concluded Millie.

Lost Lake hadn't seen so much traffic in ages, nor heard so much noise. At every remote dwelling, the trio in the truck had let loose with the "Snowplow Polka" over the megaphone. As they descended upon each home, the accumulating cars and trucks rolled down their windows and the occupants sang along and honked horns to the pulsing response, "push, push, shove, shove, beep, beep."

"We heard ya comin' a mile away!" shouted Fred and Adelaide to the musical entourage. Already dressed to go, the couple hopped into their idling car and joined the parade.

❄

Helmuth Trost was sitting in his squad car in the parking lot of the Upper Mainz public park. From this vantage point he could see if the drivers on the highway were being cautious enough at the turnoff for the Winneboujou Casino. He liked to park here, across from the casino in plain sight, to remind all travelers to pay attention to posted regulations. *Why would*

Snowplow Polka

anyone go out after a blizzard to tempt fate at a gambling den? It's inconceivable, he thought.

At some point, while watching the brake lights and the out-of-towners try to make it into the casino's snow-packed parking lot, he started to think he heard music. He turned to look out his passenger-side window.

"Well I'll be hog-tied and hornswoggled!" he said, and whistled.

Ollie and Millie's familiar snowplow was coming down the highway blaring music from its PA system so loudly that Helmuth could hear it with his windows closed. If that wasn't enough, the truck was being followed by a line of other local cars and trucks whose owners he knew well.

As the parade passed, Helmuth dropped the squad car into drive and came up behind the last vehicle—Kenny and Myrtle Rudberg's Dodge Durango. He switched on his flashing red and blue lights and gave his siren a quick blast. Neither the Rudbergs nor anyone else in the group saw these things as indications that they should pull over. Instead, the Durango's occupants turned and gave Helmuth a cheerful wave. He sighed and settled in as the caboose to their train of lively celebrants.

The sheriff wasn't exactly sure what he expected to happen after that. The raucous convoy was creating something of a hazard, or at least a distraction, but if they all stopped at the side of the road it would make one hell of a mess right in front of the Winneboujou Casino.

The plow truck turned left onto Ash Street and headed for the community center. All the others followed, and so did Helmuth, who was beginning to realize that in addition to the live music streaming from the bullhorn, the other vehicles were honking in a rhythm at even intervals. He was pleased

Dust Off Your Lederhosen

to see the community center come into view, with its neatly plowed lot. But the plow truck, instead of turning in, made a right on Maple, and then the whole polka train paraded up Main Street. Over the reverberating accordion music, Millie Reinhart's distinctive voice invited one and all to attend the holiday polka dance, "Starting right now!"

Up Main, right on Pine, back on Polk, then right again on Maple, the caravan had taken in the whole village with a show that hovered between campaign blitz and victory lap.

Helmuth realized too late that he had been seen as part of these shenanigans, following along behind and adding a kind of official seal of approval to the parade. *So, what the hell. If I can't beat 'em, I'll join 'em.* Helmuth kept his lights flashing and added his siren to the repeated two-note refrain of honks.

Some folks from town were already waiting in their cars for the festivities to begin, so when the plow and its followers entered the community center parking lot, another rollicking cacophony of horn honking blared out a greeting.

"Push, push, shove, shove, beep, beep!"

Snowplow Polka

Excited to share his new composition with the Christmas polka dance revelers, Reggie quickly unpacked his musical instruments and gear. The crowd, however, was perfectly content to spend the first quarter hour organizing the potluck dishes, exclaiming about the blizzard and hooting over all the quaint dance outfits the group had come gussied-up in.

The one-man band turned on the mic and, amid the initial feedback, delivered greetings to the polka crowd.

"Welcome, members of the Upper Mainz Polka Club! I want to thank all of you for braving the elements this evening. Also, special thanks should go to Ollie Rolloff and Millie Reinhart for plowing out a lot of snowbound comrades,

Snowplow Polka

including me. In honor of their heroic exploits, I wrote a new polka tune!" Reggie ran his fingers over the buttons and keys, dashing out an exciting trill, and then rallied the dancers. "I want the whole polka club out on the floor! Instead of opening with my usual Christmas medley, let's hear it for the 'Snowplow Polka'!"

> Let's all do the snowplow polka!
> Push, push, shove, shove, beep, beep! . . .

The wooden floor, painted with basketball court lines, was soon packed with dancers. After the chorus's yodeling introduction, Reggie called out, "Conga line! Conga line! Everybody get in line! Now . . ."

> Let's all do the snowplow polka!
> Push, push, shove, shove, beep, beep!

The dancers hopped along in the standard polka half-step, their hands placed on the hips of the person in front of them. When the beeping, shoving, plowing responses sounded, the jubilant group switched to a bumping, chugging motion that jostled the whole troupe. And when the comic verses about the intrepid rescuers rang out, they swayed and kicked to the side, like can-can dancers wending their way around the community center.

> Oh da peoples was so frightened,
> they closed der doors to hide.
> But not that good old Ollie—
> grabbed his plow 'n' took a ride.

Snowplow Polka

Happy smiles showed Reggie that his composition had been well received—he was certain that another great mixer had been added to his repertoire. Building on this spontaneous wave of excitement, he then went right into the "Merry Christmas Polka" and followed it with the "Christmas in Chicago Polka." After this high-stepping trio of tunes, it was time to cool everyone off with the evening's first slow dance, the "On the Lake Waltz." Three fast dances in a row made for enough action for most members of this old-time music crowd.

It was always charming to see how many couples stayed on the dance floor for these slow numbers. Many elderly lovebirds were no doubt transported back to bygone decades, when they had first heard these nostalgic ballads. Some were celebrating a lifetime of shared memories, and other diehard believers were still searching for the spark of new love that could stoke the heart at any age.

While Reggie brought the slow waltz to an end, he made a somber announcement. "Now we'll take a break folks, so settle on down to your tables. I know it's sad, but the time has come for the roll call of our dear members who have gone on this year to Polka Heaven. I'd like to ask Lucille Carlson, president of the club, to join me on stage to perform this duty."

The reading of the names was a melancholy observance at the holiday dance that, sad as it might be, was among the most anticipated of the evening—the commemoration always proceeded the unveiling of the food. The prayer for the departed would seamlessly meld into a blessing for the repast which they were about to receive.

After each name, the group's president added some personal details about that member and then paused for reflection. Reggie played a slow and deeply muted rendition of the

Snowplow Polka

"Battle Hymn of the Republic" on his accordion for as long as it took to complete the list.

By the time Lucille had reached the name Lars Moller, she was having a hard time maintaining her composure. Her voice trembled as she recalled that "Lars was the only dance club member to serve as treasurer for three years in a row."

"I'm sure he's helping St. Peter balance the books," Morty Mortensen whispered to Ollie.

"Yah, are you sure you sent in your dues last year?"

"Rutger Schuster. All us ladies will miss his gallant style and fancy footwork on the dance floor," Lucille lamented. "There will be no stepping on toes tonight gentlemen, because Rutger will be looking down from heaven and keeping his eye on all of you."

"And now, the last of our dear departed, Gerda Vogel. You might remember that her Wild Rice Turkey Supreme was our casserole contest winner just last year. Now she's joined her husband, Arne, at God's table."

Millie wiped away a tear and sighed, "And she was only eighty-two. Gerda was a senior when I was a freshman. She married Arne right after high school graduation."

"Could that list be any sadder?" May Grittner asked.

"Only if I were on it," her husband replied.

When all of the departed had been eulogized, the assembly quietly sang the last line of the hymn's refrain, "Glory, glory. Hallelujah. His truth is marching on."

Reggie let the final notes float among the red and green crepe paper ribbons and blinking Christmas lights, and then switched right into a lively rendition of "When the Saints Go Marching In." No one danced to this spirit-lifting anthem, but all who were able rose to clap along and sing the rousing farewell.

Snowplow Polka

After the last loud clap, Reggie raised his hand. "Hallelujah! Now it's time to eat! But . . . I have one last message before you charge over to the buffet. Tonight, Ollie Rolloff, our snowplow rescuer, will have the honor of choosing this evening's winning hot dish."

Proudly, Ollie walked over to the banquet table, took a bow and then surveyed the spectacular food laid out before him.

All of the tinfoil lids had been drawn back to reveal an array of hot dish hall-of-famers. The ladies had obviously made their best efforts on these cherished concoctions. The Christmas season always brought out the heirloom recipes—low-salt and fat-free guidelines were disregarded for once, and full-bodied flavors brought back sweet memories of holidays past. From these delicacies, the hot dish committee had already selected three finalists to compete for the blue ribbon.

A hush fell over the crowd, and Reggie whispered dramatically, "Will the ladies whose hot dishes were selected for this final round, please come forward. Members of the audience, hold your applause while the judging takes place."

The sturdy vessels containing the casseroles were often veterans themselves, as unbeatable as the recipe classics they cradled. The rectangular Pyrex dish in which Lucille Carlson had forged Italian meatball lasagna was no doubt once spotlessly clear. Now, the intrepid crucible looked as though it had scooped lava from the heart of Vesuvius for so many decades that even sandblasting couldn't bring a shine back to the glass.

"Oh my God! Lucille's lasagna is up first," Millie gasped. "Somebody better get her a chair before she falls over."

Snowplow Polka

As Ollie walked past the untouched banquet, the best that Fillmore County had to offer, he sensed that all eyes were following his progress. Trying to mimic a judge's lofty air of neutrality, he paced, with his hands behind his back, spending some time hovering over each presentation.

Connie Smaland's Chinese hamburger noodle hot dish, still nearly bubbling, was topped with a perfectly toasted crust. Her Corning Ware cube showed a bronzed patina of baked-on history. Its faithful companion, a sturdy glass lid, leaned dutifully at its side. Here was a partner whose multiple chips bespoke several nose dives to the bottom of a cast iron sink.

"Con . . . Connie's gonna win, I just know it," Myrtle Rudberg stammered.

"She represents our table," Kenny said, pumping his first. "Go Connie!"

"Quiet please. Quiet! The judge is nearing his decision," Reggie admonished. He got out a handkerchief and blotted his forehead. "The tension's building! What will it be?"

Violet Nelson's enchilada hot dish cast an odoriferous spell that would break any juror's vow of unbiased appraisal. Ollie hoped to appear blithe in the presence of this masterpiece, but he was certain his knees were quaking. Mexican fare was once as rare as hen's teeth at these northwoods gatherings, but over several decades these recipes had made deep inroads on the potluck circuit. And it was now a rare Wisconsinite who had not journeyed south of the border, at least to Texas or Arizona, on a snowbird vacation. These brave voyagers returned with fantastic tales of heavily spiced vittles that tested their intestines, then conquered their hearts.

In Violet's speciality, the stuffed tortillas nestled in a rich ocher broth beneath a melted Velveeta quilt, singed brown just inside the rim. The metal pan that hosted this distinguished

Snowplow Polka

foreigner was a time-honored ambassador of many such affairs. It had suffered numerous dueling scars, but never been pierced.

Violet sensed that the blue ribbon was within her grasp. She stepped forward, serving spoon in hand, "May I scoop you some enchilada, Mr. Rolloff?"

As in a dream, Ollie saw his plate rise with trembling hands, "Yes please. I'll have two scoops."

Violet curtsied, and the community center resounded with applause.

❄

Soon the rest of the guests at Millie and Ollie's table of eight followed his example and loaded their plates at the buffet. Kenny and Myrtle Rudberg went for the Italian meatball lasagna. Sam and May Grittner tried the No Peek Casserole.

"What've you got there, Sam?" Morty asked.

"Looks like stew meat to me, in mushroom soup," Sam replied.

"You musta peeked!" Morty gave a hardy laugh.

"And what's that exotic puff pastry dish you have, Morty?" May inquired.

"Spam Wellington."

Millie addressed the group: "I gotta say these Swedish meatballs are the best I've ever eaten."

"You do have a taste for the Scandinavians," teased Myrtle.

Sitting at the far end of the table, Connie rounded out the dinner conversation, "This is the only time I ever get to eat Seven Layer Casserole. I'd never make this at home."

In no time, Ollie had munched his way through the Mexican enchiladas and then gone back for a culinary trip to the exotic East. Chow Mein looked like a delightful place to start.

Snowplow Polka

Having returned to his place, Ollie was inhaling the aroma from his steaming plate when a sound from across the table caught his attention. He looked over to see Sam tapping a fork against the side of his glass. Sam's mouth was curled into a devilish grin, and when their eyes met, Sam twitched his eyebrows and rolled his fork like Groucho's cigar. Ollie knew he shouldn't turn around and stare at whatever Sam was gawking at, so he performed an elaborate, slow-motion pantomime: He patted his mouth, folded his napkin and carefully placed it on the table, and then leaned back and nonchalantly turned to look at the dance floor. Among the few couples now on the maple boards, the elusive Nils Helgeson had suddenly appeared, squiring the most eye-popping damsel in the room, Audrey Delcanto.

"That Chinese hot dish must be packed with spicy peppers," Sam needled. "You're as red as a beet, Ollie!"

Crossing her arms over her chest, Millie harrumphed.

May saw an opportunity to stir up some mischief. "Woohoo, take a look at the northwoods Romeo, Connie! That Nils Helgeson has to be one of the handsomest studs ever bred in Fillmore County."

"Oh, May, how can you go on like that? Nils is almost seventy—he could be my father for God's sake," Connie retorted.

May poked Connie on the arm. "I bet you make sure his mail always comes special delivery, right?"

Myrtle chuckled uncomfortably and said, "He might be a farmer, but Nils really does wear wonderfully tailored suits. Don't you love that satin trim on his western shirt?"

"And how about those Tony Lama cowboy boots, girls?" May drawled. "He paid a pretty penny for that snake skin."

Ollie took the opportunity to dispel any confusion there might be about his fashion sense. "I've got some pretty nice

Snowplow Polka

dancing clothes, too. It wasn't my idea to come here dressed in shorts when it's twenty below outside."

Kenny came to his defense. "That's right. We all wore traditional outfits tonight. It's something we do to celebrate the holidays."

"Who the heck wears rattlesnake boots to a Christmas polka dance?" Sam scoffed.

"I guess someone who would bring a woman in a tight red dress," Myrtle answered as she rose from the table and summoned the ladies, "I want to congratulate Violet on her winning hot dish. Let's go get her recipe."

❄

Morty returned to the table with a round of beer for the guys. Now that the women were gone, the four men sat back and watched the action on the dance floor. The dashing couple, Nils and Audrey, spun by to the tune of the "Tick-Tock Polka." Audrey gave a friendly wave to the men at the table.

Sam ribbed his friend. "I think that was for you, Ollie. She must have a thing for lederhosen."

"Don't make trouble, Sam," Ollie warned.

Sam continued to prod. "I guess I was just thinking that Nils might need some help handling that back forty." He then turned to Morty and said, "Maybe he would be interested in purchasing one of those newfangled 9560s, eh Morty?"

Morty scowled at Sam. "I thought we agreed to keep that a secret. Telling you anything is as good as broadcasting it on Radio KORN. I should have known better."

"What do you mean by that? I haven't said a thing."

"Then how come you asked me about that 9560 John Deere tractor, blabbermouth?"

Snowplow Polka

With curiosity aroused, Kenny leaned in. "Nobody around here needs one of those giant tanks. That baby's got 560 horsepower, doesn't it Morty?"

Morty grimaced. "This isn't about tractors, it's about something I shared with Sam the other day. But he wasn't supposed to talk about it."

"Oh come on, Morty," Sam pleaded. "It's just us guys here. Spill the beans."

All four men were now in a huddle over the table. Ollie cupped his ear so as not to miss anything.

Morty took a deep breath then exhaled and spoke. "You all know my nephew, Jason, who works at Radio Shack?"

"Yah, over in Lichtenstein," Kenny said.

Morty nodded. "That's him. Well, once in awhile he sees some very private information on people's personal computers when they get brought into the store for repairs. Jason tells me that he knows more about some guys from looking at their computers than their doctors or wives do."

"Get to the point, Morty," Ollie said, hoping the ladies wouldn't come back too soon. "What's the doggone secret here?"

"Last month Nils brought in his laptop cuz it froze up," Morty continued. "Jason told him those glitches usually come from visiting unsafe websites and not having your virus protection up to date."

"So what're you saying?" Kenny hounded.

"So Nils didn't want to leave the computer at the store—he acted kinda nervous. But Jason said he couldn't get to it that day."

"For God's sake, man, out with it!" Sam exploded. "Tell 'em what Jason saw!"

Snowplow Polka

"When he jump-started the laptop back to life . . ."

"Rebooted," Sam corrected.

Morty bristled. "Now who's interrupting? So . . . there on one side of the screen were pictures of John Deere tractors, the biggest ones too, the 9 Series . . ." He paused for effect. "On the other side were dozens of pictures of naked ladies."

Just then, two hands pressed on Ollie's shoulders and he nearly jumped out of his skin. "What are you men snickering about?" Millie asked as the ladies returned to the table. "Time to get back into the action—Reggie's gonna play "Too Fast Tommy." Come on, men. Grab your partners and hit the floor."

The "Too Fast Tommy Polka" always got the Upper Mainz Polka Club out on the dance floor, jumping and singing. Men spun their partners while the women flounced in their petticoats. When Reggie sang "Mama thinks Tommy is much too fast," all the men in the dance hall slapped their thighs and shouted, "Papa thinks he's too slow." The women then replied "Mama says Tommy should stop, stop, stop." Then the men roared back, "But Papa says go, go, go!"

> I am just an innocent lass,
> only a baby doe.
> But Papa is telling me yah, yah, yah,
> While Mama says no, no, no!

When the song neared its conclusion, Ollie felt a strong bump from behind, which caused him to bounce into Millie.

"Oops, sorry!" a lyrical high-pitched voice rang out.

Ollie and Millie turned to see who had collided with them and beheld Nils and Audrey, smirking apologetically.

In the lull between songs, the attractive couple engaged them in light chitchat.

Snowplow Polka

"How are you folks?" Nils inquired. "Ollie, I hear you're in the snowplowing business."

"We both are. We're partners," Millie informed him.

"I bet Nils would love to talk to you more about that," Audrey purred. "He just loves heavy equipment."

Ollie coughed nervously. "We drive a pretty sizable truck alright, but I can handle it."

"I bet you can," Audrey replied enticingly. "Why don't we switch partners for the next dance and you can give me the details on how your business venture is going."

Ollie hesitated, too embarrassed to speak. When he heard Reggie begin the opening cords to the slow waltz "Rhinestones Along the Rhine," he reached over and grabbed Millie's hand. "I'd love to, Audrey, but maybe another time—this is our song."

"Sure, another time," Audrey said. "Nils is due for a smoke break anyways."

Millie and Ollie slipped seamlessly into each other's arms, and the swell of the opening chorus carried them into a spin.

> She wore rhinestones along the Rhine.
> How those baubles did sparkle and shine.
> Though a rich man could place
> true gems 'round her face,
> my love wore rhinestones along the Rhine.
>
> We walked down the wide promenade
> while moonbeams on river waves played.
> I said, "I can't give you real diamonds,
> you'd laugh if you knew what I paid."

Snowplow Polka

Then Reggie swooned and switched to his high falsetto, which he did whenever the lyrics represented the girl answering her impoverished suitor.

> "Mein Liebchen," she sighed, oh so tender,
> "do you think that my heart is for sale?
> Your gift I will always remember
> as the true star that never will fail."

> "Yah, those rich boys can play with their money,
> and flip silver coins at my heart.
> But these rhinestones you give me, my honey,
> are enough to ensure I won't part.

> When our grandchildren look at my treasures,
> they will ask, Nana, dear, are they real?'
> I will think of my life and its pleasures,
> Yah, on my heart they were pressed like a seal."

The chorus was sung one final time, and the dancers slowly spun to a stop. Millie and Ollie looked into each other's eyes and exchanged a brief kiss. Not quite ready to spring into the "Chipmunk Song," Reggie's next polka ditty, they made their way back to the table.

Just as they reached their seats, Lucille Carlson came rushing over anxiously. "Did you bring the punch bowl set, Millie? I was hoping to get everything arranged tonight for tomorrow's meeting."

Millie's confusion morphed into shock. "Egads, the punch bowl! I had so many things on my mind today, Lucille! I even got it off the shelf in the basement and put it on the backseat of the Buick. Good heavens, I'm sorry."

Snowplow Polka

Lucille looked truly panicked. She rubbed her upper arms and shuddered with nervous frustration. "The Indian Head county clerks are all meeting at my office first thing in the morning. I wanted to have the refreshment table all set and ready to go. Oh my, oh my."

"Ollie could bring the punch bowl to your office first thing in the morning. He could even help you get things ready."

"Oh no, I always do it the night before," Lucille insisted. "They only come to Upper Mainz twice a year. I just couldn't sleep if I didn't know everything was in its place, everything just right—you know. Not that I don't trust Ollie, of course."

Millie turned to Ollie for assistance. She had that plan-of-action look that meant the upcoming request was actually an order. "Ollie?" she began, in a pleading voice. "Would you run home and get the punch bowl for Lucille? When we had to use the plow truck today, I just totally forgot about that thing being in the Park Avenue."

Before Ollie could reply, much less object, Millie added new evidence of the logic of her proposal. "It would be so much better if you came back with the car. Reggie would be more comfortable, and there would be more room for his instruments. Honestly, I don't know if I could climb into that truck one more time after a day of plowing and a night of dancing."

Game, set, and match—before I even got in a swing, thought Ollie. "OK, babe. I'll go get the punch bowl and come back in the Buick. You're right, there's more room in the car for Reggie's gear, too."

Millie and Lucille beamed angelically at their hero as he headed toward the coat rack out in the hallway. In the background, Ollie heard the first strains of the "Happy Bachelor Polka" as he slipped into his parka. He didn't feel like climbing

Snowplow Polka

into his snowmobile pants again, but was taking them off the hook when the outside door behind him slammed.

"Mr. Rolloff," Audrey said, "you aren't leaving already, are you?"

"Ah, . . . well, Audrey, ah . . . I have to run home and get something we forgot. I *am* coming back."

"We?" The interrogator latched onto the key confessional word.

"Yes, me and ah . . . Millie. We live together." This clarification, which Ollie thought would make him sound unavailable, instead pricked her interest.

"So, you're not married?"

Ollie felt his head shaking back and forth.

"You're cohabitating out of wedlock? How avant-garde."

Finding his voice, Ollie asked, "And where's your partner, Nils? Still smoking?"

"He's out warming up the car. I forgot my boots and came back in to get them."

"So, you're leaving early, too? I guess that means we won't get that spin around the dance floor this year," Ollie teased.

"Oh, you caught me there. It looks like we'll have to wait for that pleasure," Audrey cooed as she retrieved her boots from under the coat rack. "Could you help me with the zippers on these? It's so hard to bend over in this tight dress."

When Ollie stood up after zipping her boots, Audrey took his arm and asked, "Will you escort me to the door?"

With a broad grin, Ollie consented, and they walked together toward the exit. As he leaned against the handle to open the door, a whoosh of frigid air rushed up his lederhosen.

Night Patrol

The entire solitary ride home, Ollie's mind was alive with mixed emotions. Outside, enormous snowflakes floated in near suspension before the truck's high beams while he replayed the evening's events. His awkward encounter with Audrey had given his blood pressure a little rise. As he drove the darkened roadways, this vision began to fade and the reality of his circumstances brought him back down to earth. Every dance group probably has an Audrey, someone to add some spice to the evening's entertainment and set the tongues to wagging. Yet, when all was said and done, most couples were happy to head home together, secure in the knowledge that they had a long-term partner to dance with.

Snowplow Polka

You're pretty damn lucky to have a lady like Millie, Ollie told himself. *You've been a bachelor your whole life, but now you're with someone special. She loves you, took you into her home, and her kids think you're OK, so Rolloff, don't mess up this good deal.*

❄

By the time he passed the intersection of 14½ and 2¼, the truck seemed to be driving itself along the familiar dead-end road. The night's flurries had left a quarter-inch of sparkling snow on the gravel, and as Ollie approached the top of his driveway he noticed fresh tire tracks in the new snow. Slowly, he turned into the driveway and stopped. From this vantage point, before the drive dipped down, Ollie could see the trail leading right to their garage. He noticed, with a touch of fear, that there was a bare patch of gravel between the tire tracks, which meant that a vehicle had idled there for some time very recently, melting the snow.

Who would've been here? Ollie wondered. *Was someone looking for us? A friend? That doesn't make sense—everyone knows we'd be at the Christmas dance. The kids? Did they come early? I doubt it. They know our schedule, and they would've gotten out to test the door, or even gone in—they have a key.*

He felt a little vulnerable sitting there alone, looking at their home. But he gripped the steering wheel and bent forward to study the scene more carefully. *Tread marks, but no footprints—that's a good sign.*

Ollie proceded slowly down the driveway and pressed the garage door opener. The right-hand door slid open and the light came on. The empty interior space seemed to be normal. He could see nothing missing or out of place, but he still

Night Patrol

had the jitters. Parking the truck outside, he got out and cautiously walked into the garage. Everything still looked fine—the Buick was on the other side, and nothing looked like it had been touched. Ollie felt like just hopping into the car and charging away, but he thought he'd better at least stick his head into the house.

Not wanting to turn on lights that would expose his movements to any intruder, he walked down the hallway and past the kitchen in the dark. In the combined dining and living room, faint shadows from trees outside made ghostly shapes on the squat forms of the furniture. Ollie wondered if he should call out, but that seemed silly.

Should I notify the sheriff? What would I report? No one's been inside—a car only turned around in the drive. I'll tell Helmuth anyway when I get back to the dance.

Returning to the garage, Ollie double-checked the house door to make sure it was locked. He decided to leave the truck parked outside to make it look like someone was home and closed the garage door. Then he went to the Buick, moved the punch bowl set from the backseat to the floor, and cleared out the trunk space so there would be room for Reggie's instruments. As the left garage door rolled up, Ollie let out a long breath and started to relax.

But just as he dropped the car into reverse a human form appeared in the rearview mirror. Ollie felt his spine stiffen and the hair on his neck rise. *Close the door or make a run for it?* His hands went clammy as he stomped on the gas and sent the Buick flying backward from its cave like a bat out of hell.

The person in the driveway leapt to the side just in time and was so close to the car that Ollie thought he heard a metallic ping on the Park Avenue's fender. In a panic, he slammed

Snowplow Polka

on the brakes, causing the punch bowl and glasses to tinkle in their box. When he looked over the dashboard, he saw the intruder step into the car's headlights.

"Oh my God!" Ollie yelled when he identified the hulking figure covered in camouflage gear and animal pelts. "Amos! What the hell are you doing?"

At the same time, Amos shouted, "Stop! Stop!" as he advanced toward the Buick, holding both of his hands up to reinforce his order.

Ollie's pounding heart slowed slightly, and he quickly got out of the car.

"Amos, are you alright? Did I hit you? Are you ok?"

His wooly neighbor spoke breathlessly. "There've been strangers in the area. I think they were watching your house. I thought I saw their car driving past the Gustafsons', too."

Ollie tried to judge Amos's mental state. Instead of talking in biblical riddles, he sounded clear-headed and genuinely concerned. Then it hit him: "It might be the cabin robbers the sheriff's been having so much trouble with!" he exclaimed.

"I think I've seen the car before, cruising in the area—two guys in an old green four-door driving slow. Made me suspicious."

Ollie nodded. "Yah, back in November, when we were plowing, after that first snowfall, Millie and I saw two guys parked in a closed rest stop. They had guns in the car. I reported it to the sheriff."

"I heard about that. It's gotta be the same guys."

"I have to get back into town to get Millie and Reggie at the dance," Ollie said excitedly. "I'm sure Helmuth will still be there. I'll let him know what you've seen. We all have to be careful."

Night Patrol

"Good plan, sir!" The addled vet replied, standing at attention and presenting a crisp salute. "I'll be on guard duty all night."

The lone sentry marched off, now bent over slightly, his head pivoting from side to side. As Ollie watched the phantom disappear into the trees, he could hear him mutter, "I wish we had more troops. This perimeter is too damn long." Ollie was relieved that Amos appeared to be traveling unarmed.

❄

The drive back seemed long, and Ollie was apprehensive. The community center parking lot was nearly empty by the time he returned. He glanced at the clock on the dashboard: *Ten after twelve. That's good.* It was too bad he had missed the last dance, but after seeing the unsettling evidence of trespassers at home and the startling encounter with Amos, he was in no mood to put on a smile.

A few of the diehard dancers were still straggling off to their cars, and over by the back steps a hardy bunch was laughing and talking loudly. He wondered if he should tell them his disturbing news, but decided that he really didn't have much to report. The evidence was certainly circumstantial, and most of these people lived in Upper Mainz, or other small towns nearby, so news of cabin burglars out in the countryside didn't affect them much. *No need to cause undue panic*, he thought.

Ollie backed right up to the door so they could load Reggie's stuff quickly. He hopped out with the punch bowl and tried to jockey his way past the dawdling crowd without stopping or saying anything. They hooted out a string of quips.

"Aren't you a little late, Ollie?"

Snowplow Polka

"Millie went home with Nils Helgeson!"

"I've heard of bringing your own bottle, but a whole punch bowl?"

In the hallway, the cold fluorescent overhead lights were now on. Ollie couldn't think of anything more unappealing than the smell of stale beer and room-temperature food combined with the sight of discarded decorations under that green glow.

Lucille was overjoyed to see him and accepted the punch bowl as if it were a trophy presented at the county fair.

"Where's the sheriff?" Ollie asked her.

"He got a 911, about an accident out on the highway," she replied.

Before Ollie could respond to that news, Reggie signaled him from across the room. "It's about time you got here. How 'bout givin' me a hand with this gear?"

While the two men rolled cords, collapsed microphones, and packed away instruments, Ollie briefed his friend on the troubling things he'd seen at home.

When Millie came out of the kitchen, Ollie heard her asking Lucille if any more help was needed. But he took her aside and tried to give her the gist of his story quickly. Millie neither overreacted nor pressed for more details. Showing her true mettle, she immediately returned to the group of ladies assigned to kitchen duty and told them that she and Ollie would have to leave right away to get Reggie home.

❆

The calm the three of them had displayed inside the community center went out the window as soon as they waved their goodbyes to the last celebrants. Crammed into the Park

Night Patrol

Avenue with some of the instruments, Millie, Ollie and Reggie began to babble like henhouse chicks who'd seen a fox.

"Somebody broke into the house!" Millie exclaimed.

"No, I only saw tire tracks in the driveway," Ollie explained.

"Did you go inside? Was anything missing?"

"I checked inside—everything looked fine."

"You said Amos saw robbers?" Reggie prodded.

"No, he saw a suspicious vehicle in the area," Ollie clarified further. "He didn't like the look of it."

"So Amos saw a car, you saw tire tracks, and the house is fine," summarized Reggie.

Millie turned and wagged her finger at the musician. "Don't go saying this ain't no big deal, Reggie. There's been a string of break-ins all around the lake."

Reggie nodded. "Damn good reasons for us all to get right home and lock our doors."

"But that don't mean we won't keep our eyes peeled on the way," she said. "Ollie and I are practically agents of the law, and we're deputizing you."

Rather than the main highway, they took the county roads and watched at each turnoff for unexpected tread marks in the new snow, especially when the roads led only to shoreline lots where there should be no activity during most of the winter season. They made it to OO and were about five miles from the turnoff to Reggie's when Ollie slowed to a crawl. All three saw the same thing and seemed to share each other's thoughts. Several sets of tire tracks had taken a right at the gravel road going to the cabins along Small Mouth Bay on Lower Bass Lake. Ollie glanced over at Millie and she at him, then they both turned to the backseat, where they could see that Reggie looked concerned, even in the near dark.

Reggie gave first testimony. "I haven't seen anyone around

Snowplow Polka

those cabins in over a month." The musician twisted the tips of his mustache anxiously.

"And this snow didn't start till about eight tonight. So who would've come here that late?" Ollie questioned.

"Do those look like the tread marks you saw at our place, Ollie?"

"What is this, *CSI*?" he replied. "I didn't go out and photograph them. All I know is, this looks suspicious."

"Yah," Millie agreed, "who would come out here this time of year and in the middle of the night?"

"Maybe we'd better contact Sheriff Trost," Reggie suggested. "I didn't see him when we left the dance."

"Lucille said he got called away to an accident. I was gonna tell him about what Amos and I saw, but since he was busy, I figured it could wait till morning," Ollie said. Then he asked Millie, "Hey, doesn't your brother Richie have a cabin here on Small Mouth Bay?"

"By God you're right, Rolloff. I haven't been there in years. It's not much more than a two-room fishing shack. I remember which one it is though—a tiny pink place off a ways from the water, with a plastic fish for a mailbox."

"Think we should check it out?"

"Does a bear go in the woods?"

"Come on you guys!" Reggie whined. "If it's robbers, they could be armed! Remember the kids who stumbled into those crooks across the lake from you back in November? They got shot at."

"We'll just take a little look-see. If there's trouble, we skedaddle out of there and call the sheriff," Millie coaxed.

Reggie moaned. "Damn, I haven't even made my last intentions known to Eli Frost yet."

"Keep your lights off and your voices down," Millie whis-

Night Patrol

pered melodramatically. "And when you're near enough, cut the engine and roll to a stop."

Ollie thought this a bit overdone, but drove ahead slowly. Even without headlights, the dark tread marks against the white ground were an easy trail to follow.

"There's at least three or four sets of tracks here," Ollie observed. "Is this a cabin robber's convention?"

"Maybe it's some damn fools who believe those tales about Richie burying his money in a strong box out here," Millie speculated.

"I never heard that."

"And I never said it, either."

Reggie prayed to his deceased wife, "Dust off a harp, Hedwig, I'm on my way."

As if on cue, all the tread marks turned off at the mailbox in the shape of a giant fish. The driveway was shared by three cabins, but all the vehicles were at the smaller pink one on the far left.

After they made the turn, Millie began to narrate the scene to her anxious but amused companions in an exaggerated whisper, pointing out the obvious: The cabin that belonged to her brother was the gathering spot. Two pickup trucks and two cars were parked in front of it. Then, to enhance the high-alert atmosphere, she quit speaking completely and switched to the quick hand signals that a raiding platoon behind enemy lines would employ.

The Park Avenue's approach was concealed by a windbreak of dense spruce trees that grew along the lot line. When the car rolled to a stop it was hidden by a red log cabin. Everyone opened their door with caution, trying not to make any noise. Once they were out in the snow, closing the doors was another matter.

Snowplow Polka

"Just leave the doors open, so there's no banging noise," Millie commanded in a dramatic undertone. "Who knows, we might have to make a quick getaway."

"I ain't leaving the doors open! The light will stay on and the battery will die," sputtered Ollie.

"We can't leave my accordions unlocked in there," added Reggie.

"OK, just try to keep the handle up when you close it and let it click, then bump it shut," directed Millie.

It was now almost one in the morning. There was definitely activity in the cabin—lots of activity! With four vehicles in front, there was no telling how many prowlers might be at the scene, so following the original plan of sneaking up and trying to get a look inside certainly seemed the wisest idea.

The pink cabin didn't allow any obvious access for spying on the interlopers inside. All the windows had shades that were tightly drawn, typical protocol for closing a seasonal lake place. The front and back doors both had windows, but they were covered with an opaque green and orange plaid fabric that blocked all views of the interior. *That looks like the quilt I gave Richie and Eunice for their twenty-fifth,* Millie thought.

Upon closer inspection, one wee crack of light could be seen near the top of a sliding glass door facing the deck. The corner of the floral bed sheet covering the window had come undone. Millie pointed to the breach and then signaled with her hand for the men to come forward. The three seniors moved hesitantly across the snow-covered wooden deck. When they made it to the door, Millie whispered, "Hoist me up."

Ollie and Reggie both rolled their eyes in disbelief and mouthed the words, "No way!"

With a huff, her hands on her hips, Millie stared at them until they relented. The men stooped over, she stepped into their cupped hands, and with one boost they heaved her into the air.

"Higher," she hissed.

The two men jostled their awkward load and tried to raise the spy a few more inches. But the human pyramid began to quiver, and Reggie, working to gain a better foothold, started to feel his left boot slide away on the now-packed snow.

"Aieeeeeee!" screamed Millie as she came tumbling down, throwing all three of them into a pile of stacked plastic outdoor furniture.

The sheet covering the window was flung back, and the glass door slid open with a thud.

A young man rushed out and saw a squirming pile of parkas, petticoats and jumbled deck chairs.

"What the hell is goin' on out here!"

"Bret?"

"Great-Aunt Millie? Is that you?"

"Who's in this house anyway?" Millie demanded. "We're on the trail of some cabin robbers. You scared the daylights out of us."

Bret considered this, chuckled and shook his head. "So, you guys want a beer?"

Rap Polka

The three polka dancers followed Millie's great-nephew into a small linoleum-floored space that served as the kitchen and dining half of the cabin's front room. Beneath a buzzing circular fluorescent tube, two guys tore scraps from a floppy pizza like crows at a roadside carcass. Rap music was thumping at a high decibel, and the air was a sweet, choking fogbank of cannabis haze. Four other boys and two girls were slouched around an enamel-top kitchen table onto which a Michigan Rummy game's boundaries had been drawn with masking tape. High penny piles on some pots indicated that the game had been dragging on for quite awhile. In the living room area, another couple leaned against each other in the corner of a tired Flexsteel sofa. They sat under a crocheted throw of psychedelic granny squares, watching car races on a muted TV.

None of them seemed to care, or even notice, that several new guests had arrived. When Bret said something to rouse their attention, not a soul responded. So he sauntered over to the source of the music and paused it. That did the trick. None of the partiers looked startled, but the groggy group raised their heads to see what had killed the tunes.

"Hey guys, this is my great-aunt Millie . . ."

"For goodness sakes, Bret," Millie interrupted. "I might be great, but I'm not that ancient! Just call me aunt!"

"Ok, so this is my Aunt Millie, and her boy- . . . ah . . . guy friend here, Ollie, and the musician Reggie VanArsdale."

"A magician?" one sleepy-eyed card player queried.

"Yah sure!" Reggie chuckled. "When I walked in, the music vanished."

The card player stroked a scraggly soul patch and looked like he was trying to figure out whether he'd been punked.

By this time the three party crashers had shed their winter coats and were facing the group in full antique dancing costume. The kids must have thought they'd been busted by the von Trapp Family Singers.

"My aunt and her posse are out searching for cabin robbers. I think they got worried when they saw lights here at my grandpa's lake place."

"Do you play polkas to scare them away?" another wit at the table ventured, to a full round of yucks and snorts.

"Hey, this is serious stuff," Bret countered. "Remember last month when those robbers surprised Garber and his girlfriend and he got a piece of his rear end shot off?"

Rap Polka

"Yah, that's one piece he'll never see again," the wit retorted.

At the back of the room, a maroon and yellow paisley print curtain that acted as a door to the bedroom began to flutter and then was slid aside. Two disheveled girls with bed hair and smeared mascara emerged. Neither was wearing pants, or anything on their feet, but an oversized UW River Falls sweatshirt on one and a man's shirt with long tails on the other kept everything decent.

"What happened to the music?" one asked, yawning.

"I paused the music to tell you guys that my aunt and her friends are here," Bret explained. "They saw lights and thought we might be cabin robbers."

"Cabin robbers!" one of the waifs giggled. "Do we look like cabin robbers?"

Ollie scanned the tottering girls and then asked one of them, "Aren't you a granddaughter of Adelaide's?"

"Uh-huh. I'm Skeeter," the girl in the sweatshirt answered.

"Skeeter? What's your real name?"

"Adelaide."

❄

Millie hobbled over to the sofa, where the couple scooted closer together to make room for her. "I hope you don't mind if I make myself at home," Millie said. "We've run all day and danced all night—I've got to rest these tired feet." She swooshed her dancing dress and crinolines forward and sat down with a poof.

"Umph, umph!" came a muffled cry from under a blanket bunched in a heap on the couch.

Instantaneously, Millie jumped back up and turned to see

Snowplow Polka

what she'd sat on. Her cheeks went crimson and she held her hands over her heart. "Oh my God! Did I just crush a dog?"

The entire room broke out into hysterical laughter while a previously unseen kid emerged from the blanket.

"Hey Stoney," a pizza muncher guffawed, "we thought you'd gone home over an hour ago."

"Looks like somebody forgot to put the dog out," a card player jested.

"Aw jeez, lady," the now visible kid said as he stood and stretched. "I'm sorry I scared you. Here, take my spot."

The young couple also got up. The boy said, "There's plenty of room for your friends, too."

As the silly hijinks subsided, a relieved Millie sat back down. A girl in a Badgers hoodie at the card table called out, "Hey Bret, turn the music back on! Let's get this party rolling!"

"OK! Let's make some noise." Bret hit a button. Speakers blared, the kitchen light flickered, and the walls reverberated with the thumping bass.

Nobody said that conversation time was over, but the wall of sound produced an atmosphere just as impenetrable as the cloudy air. The slackers all turned back to their own amusements and paid no further attention to the older people.

Millie wasn't about to say goodnight that quickly. "Bret. Hey Bret, I thought you invited us in for a beer."

"Oh yeah, man. Ollie? Hey, music man—you guys want a cold one?" Bret grabbed three cups and filled them from the keg tap.

Millie made room on the sofa for her polka companions and then asked, "Ollie, what is this kind of music?"

"Not the kind they dance to." Ollie took a slug of beer and looked around the room. "Not the kind they sing to, either."

Rap Polka

"Can you believe it?" Millie frowned. "I like music that makes me happy, gets me moving. These kids just sat back and started playing cards again. Where's the party?"

"This rap music does have a steady rhythm, but it's hard to make out the words," Reggie added.

"What are the words?" Millie asked.

The three elders concentrated on the kids' rap music.

A vulgar expletive in the lyrics caught Millie's attention. The longer she listened, the more she realized that the entire song was one never-ending string of rhyming profanity.

"What the hell is all this swearing you're listening to?" Millie boomed, surprising even herself.

Everyone turned to look at her and then over to Bret. The party host shifted uncomfortably and then dialed down the music's volume. "Come on, Aunt Millie. This is our music. I know it's not what you listen to, but we like it."

"Who made this recording? A friend of yours?" Millie demanded.

"I wishhh," the tangle-haired girl in the man's shirt said, holding the last word about two and a half times longer than necessary.

"You mean this garbage is for sale in stores?" Millie demanded. "They don't get arrested for making smut?"

Bret took a stand. "Aunt Millie, aren't you forgetting about the First Amendment?"

"Yah, I know, freedom of speech. And the damn beat never changes! It's the same thing over and over, only with nastier and nastier words."

A wiry guy with bushy rust-colored hair walked away from the rummy game and joined the conflict, "Lady, what's your problem? Chill."

Snowplow Polka

Ollie rose to his feet and patted Millie's sleeve. "Babe, it's time to get Reggie home, dontcha think?"

"What kind of music do you like?" Skeeter asked sweetly, causing the whole group to turn to see where this soft interruption came from.

Lounging against the arm of the couch the girl in shirttails said, "I like all kinds of music, don't you, Skeeter?"

Ollie smiled at the sleepy duo. "We like old-time music. We like to polka."

"Oh, I remember my grandpa teaching me that one at my cousin's wedding. He and I always had so much fun," the girl said, tugging at her shirt.

Reggie got to his feet, reenergized. "If you wanna hear some real live music, I'm your man!"

The half-dressed nymph from the couch got up and stumbled over to the seniors in her bare feet. "What's the name of your band, Reggie?" she asked while brushing the feather on his alpine hat.

"Yah, you got it."

"Huh?"

"I don't use another name—just Reggie . . . the one-man band."

"Oh wow, like Jay-Z."

"I guess so."

"Let's give these kids a treat! Run out to the car and get your accordion," Millie instructed. "Ollie, you go and help. Make sure all the doors are shut good, too."

❄

"The Bling Meister is in the house!" Bret announced after the

Rap Polka

men returned and Reggie was strapping on his dazzling instrument. "Squeeze it, Reg!"

The musician ran through a quick succession of taps and keyboard runs to loosen his fingers. Then, before the dazed viewers could gather their senses, he transitioned right into "In Heaven There Is No Beer."

Millie felt certain a little instruction was needed, so she grabbed Ollie and they twirled about in a demonstration round. There wasn't much space for maneuvering in the main room, but everyone moved back to let the couple promenade and spin.

Reggie considered lowering his volume, but then he thought, *What the heck, these kids like loud music, don't they?* He let 'er rip while the cabin's springing floorboards groaned under his friends' half-stepping feet.

The crowd clapped along, and when the song ended, a round of applause and whistles erupted from the kids.

"That's right, man! Roll out the barrel—we got a kegger goin' here!" a chubby dude in a faded black T-shirt hollered. "What about the other one like that? My mom always liked that one—"How Do You Know There Ain't No Beer in Heaven?""

One go-around was sufficient for Ollie. He dropped like a sack of potatoes onto the couch. He watched as Millie, looking for a new partner, grabbed Bret and began to teach him some steps. The kids were definitely enthused by the way-back tunes, and several were pairing off to join the dance. He couldn't really say they were doing the polka, but then again, even if they knew how, there wasn't enough space in the cabin for organized group dancing. The kids pretty much just sprang like synchronized pogo sticks in a circuit around the front room.

Snowplow Polka

The wiry boy with the bushy hair now challenged the accordion player: "Hey old man! Don't you know any rap?"

Reggie brought the polka to its signature fadeout and then acknowledged the squinting critic. "How does it go?"

The kids looked at each other, and someone said, "It's gotta rhyme, man, and the cooler the rhyme, the better the rapper you are."

Instead of pooh-poohing the kids, Reggie listened to the repetitious chant they were doing and began echoing the cadence by pumping the bellows and pressing a simple pattern on the keys.

"I'll throw out the first lines," Reggie suggested, "and you all try to follow up."

> We went down to the cabin,
> cuz we thought we saw a light.
> We were hoping for no robbers,
> cuz we didn't want a fight.

At first the group was dumbfounded by what they had heard, and it seemed that nobody would answer the accordion player's challenge. All at once, looks of amazement faded and smiles appeared.

"Wow!" one kid exclaimed.

"Even an old dude can rap," Stoney said as he smacked his forehead.

The wiry boy agreed. "You can make up your own words. Hell, man, you can rap about whatever." At that point he strutted in front of the crowd and began to rap.

> We were pissed about the geezers,
> cuz they busted up our game.

Rap Polka

> We were laughin' at their outfits,
> cuz they were lookin' pretty lame.

Next the chubby kid took center stage, grinding his hips and stirring the air with a pointed finger. He was good at entertaining the crowd while buying time to devise his own verses.

> Then they started with the polka,
> and were steppin' on the gas.
> We were cruisin' with the oldies,
> and it shook my happy ass.

Reggie got the feeling that these slightly raunchy lyrics might degenerate and the whole song would lapse into profanity. He hoped he could break the kid's rhythm and give someone else a chance to contribute new lines. The accordion player made a quick adjustment and switched to 2/4 polka time.

> Rap—We do the rap rap polka!
> Dance—beneath the cold full moon.
> Rap—We do the rap rap polka.
> Home—we're gonna be there soon.

Sure enough, the naughty rap lost its momentum, and the chubby kid couldn't find his way back into the groove. He was still gyrating, but now he wobbled like a top about to tumble off its axis.

Without warning the cabin door crashed open and Helmuth Trost launched himself into the room. "Freeze!" he yelled. "Nobody make a move!"

Snowplow Polka

The sheriff was decked out in full uniform with a shiny badge pinned front and center on his fur trooper hat. He had his Glock drawn, aiming it left and right to cover the whole room.

"Holy shit!" everyone shrieked.

Smite the Robbers

"I thought the sheriff's jaw was gonna hit the floor when he spotted us!" Reggie howled.

The Buick shook with the laughter of the three seniors as they made their way home from the busted party.

"My poor grandnephew Bret thought he was gonna have a private Christmas bash with his buddies. Now he's gonna be the laughingstock of the town!" Millie squealed.

Ollie chimed in: "And what are they gonna say at the Cowbell when they hear we fell into a pile of lawn chairs trying to peek into your brother's cabin?"

"Maybe they'll forget that when they hear Millie sat on a kid and thought he was a dog!" Reggie said between guffaws.

Snowplow Polka

All the way to Reggie's house, just when it seemed the three would get over their silliness, someone would begin to recount another one of the outlandish episodes from the evening. Before they could even finish, the Park Avenue would start to rock again as they completed each other's tales.

"You saved the dance, Ollie! You saved the day!" was Reggie's last tribute as he stumbled through newly fallen snow up the front porch steps to his house. "That was one Christmas party I'll never forget!"

Millie waved goodbye. "We'll be thinkin' about you when we do our Christmas rap!"

She and Ollie headed home, running on adrenaline—and punchy gags interspersed with bogus accusations and intimate flirtations.

"You really gave those kids a piece of your mind about their taste in music, babe," Ollie chuckled. "By the time the night was over we'd won some polka converts."

Millie couldn't suppress a yawn. Smiling, though, she said, "We've got to get some sleep. Rick and Vicky will be here before noon. There're gonna think we're a couple of all-night carousers if we're not out of bed and dressed when they get here. Tomorrow is Christmas Eve Day, you know."

"Tomorrow? You mean today—it's already four in the morning, and the snow is really starting to come down again.

"The weatherman didn't predict this," Millie agreed.

"We'll be lucky if we get to open gifts before it's time to plow. Good thing we're almost home." He drove through the canyons of plowed snow along 2¼, past the fields of Gustafson's farm. The sleepiness was contagious, and Ollie's face was stretched into a wide yawn when a sharp flash of light exploded before his eyes and sent a kaleidoscope of floating spheres into his dilated pupils.

Smite the Robbers

"What's that light?" Millie wailed.

The two struggled to focus their throbbing eyes as they squinted through raised forearms and spread fingers. Dazzling shafts of light began to bear down on them.

"That's our truck!" Millie cried with fear and anger. "Some bastard is stealing our truck!"

"I can't see the road!" Ollie shouted.

The car began to slide. Ollie pumped the brakes repeatedly, but the tires failed to find traction against the icy roadway. The deep ditch, loaded with an ocean of snow, fell off sharply just a few feet away.

The charging snowplow dropped its blade, and a shower of sparks from struck gravel added to the nightmarish sight. The high-angled blade coming right at them with its wave of thrown snow was the last thing the hapless couple could see. In a terrifying instant, the Park Avenue went up an embankment, then dipped sharply and did a complete side-over-side roll. The world beyond their cracking windshield went from a tunnel of white light to the black nothingness of a tomb.

❄

The marauding snowplow lurched to a shuddering halt, and Jedidiah's head slammed back against the passenger side headrest.

"Jesus, Hank! Where the hell did you learn to drive?" He shook off the jolt then turned to look out at the crash scene, twitching nervously and readjusting the visor of his red-and-black checked hat. "Back it up, man. I can't believe we blew those geezers right off the road."

"Take it easy there, Jedidiah," the driver cautioned as he put the truck into reverse. He wanted to get a better look at

Snowplow Polka

their handiwork, too, but then saw trouble as his agitated partner opened the window and brought out a .30-06 rifle that he had stowed beneath the seat. "Keep that hardware hidden," Hank commanded with an ominous drawl.

Jedidiah kept fidgeting with the gun, but Hank's hand, the size of a bear paw, grabbed his forearm and closed like a vise.

"I said, take it easy, Jed. No need for that."

"I think I see right where they went in. Damn! We buried those two stiffs!"

The wake from the charging snowplow had put a fresh white frosting over the scene of the crime. The crash site lay hidden in an anonymous ditch. All evidence of the Buick and its occupants had been swept away.

"I'm gonna pump some lead into that pile right there. That's where they went down," Jed sputtered.

The burly driver wouldn't relinquish his grip on his sidekick. Hank spoke with the solemn calm of an adult addressing a four-year-old: "Jed, we only came here to steal a truck. I think you know the difference between robbery and murder."

"But I think we already murdered them. I just want to make sure."

"What happened was an accident. The law could never prove intent. By the time they dig those two up, we'll be long gone. We can unload this truck in the Cities, no questions asked, and be on our way to Margaritaville."

When the driver was satisfied that his partner had stowed the weapon and that no movement or sound could be detected coming from the undistinguished snowbank, he exhaled with finality and turned his attention once again to the road ahead.

"What the hell is that?" Hank gasped in alarm.

The vision before him turned his sigh of relief into a choked exclamation. Directly in their path was a lone horseman etched

Smite the Robbers

in harsh detail by the truck's floodlights. The mounted apparition, cloaked in animal pelts, had in his hand a twin-barrel shotgun pointed directly at them. His oversized horse snorted while digging its shag-covered hooves into the snow.

The specter's mouth opened to speak, and a puff of mist billowed out to cling to his hoar-frosted beard. Hank lowered his window to hear the command.

"I said, turn off your engine and put your hands up, or I'll pump ya full of buckshot."

"Why'd you tell me to put the gun away?" Jedidiah hissed.

"Keep your trap shut," Hank whispered back. "I'm gonna drop this thing in reverse and try to quick raise the blade. Then you grab your gun."

"He'll shoot us, man!" the quivering guy whined, a bit too loudly.

"I think he'll be scared to pull the trigger."

"You *think*? Aw shit, man!"

Hank slammed the gear shift into reverse and pressed the gas pedal to the floor.

Amos did indeed hesitate, stunned by the bastard's audacity. The truck heaved and then began backing away from him.

"You bettin' I won't do it? Eat lead ya pissant thieves!" Amos yelled. He let go with both barrels, and the gun spewed a shower of sparks and buckshot at the fleeing truck. The blade had gotten high enough to protect part of the cab, but not all of it, and the windshield shattered in place, becoming an opaque web of cracks that made seeing through it nearly impossible. The shot also took out the right headlight and the roof-mounted flood lamp while leaving the hood as pockmarked as the moon.

The F-250 rumbled back down the driveway, coming dangerously close to Ollie and Millie's house before Hank spun the

Snowplow Polka

wheel and jammed the truck into drive. The fugitives drove past the home and plowed through the drifted yard toward Little Butternut Lake.

"The ice ain't thick enough yet! It won't support this monster truck, Hank!" Jedidiah cried as they careened toward the frozen expanse.

"It'll hold if the truck keeps rolling!" Hank bellowed as he stuck his head out the side window to see more clearly. "I'll drive across the lake and onto the highway at the other end. We can't let that damn nut on a horse get close to us again. We may not be so lucky next time!"

The plow truck sped up a gentle hill and through Millie's terraced flower beds, demolishing the prized roses slumbering under a blanket of snow. There was a particularly violent sound of tearing metal as the vehicle raced over the beached dock, leaving crushed aluminum and wood planks behind and slowing their escape.

"You're not gonna get away that easy," said Amos as he quickly reloaded his gun and watched the truck make a mess of Millie's garden. His blood was boiling, and even Titus seemed hot to charge. The lumbering Belgian hadn't flinched at the sound of the gun going off, and he whinnied, signaling his willingness to join in the hunt.

"You ready to charge, Titus? We're goin' into battle against evil."

The great beast shook his mane in approval.

"Watch your footing, my trusty steed. Stick to the snowmobile trail. We're gonna cut 'em off."

As Amos watched in amusement, the large truck spun and fishtailed, its chunky tires burning through the snow to lake ice. But he could also see that the man on the passenger side now had a rifle in his hands.

Smite the Robbers

Giving the reins a tug to the left, Amos barked a string of commands: "Stay on the driver's side. Don't let that guy get a shot. Keep him blocked."

Amos was in no position to do much shooting himself—he could barely hang onto the large horse and his shotgun at the same time. But he kept the firearm out in plain sight and could see it was spooking the driver.

From the time the truck had hit the frozen lake, enormous groaning sighs began emanating from beneath the sheet.

Titus closed on the driver's side door, herding the truck with continual pressure on the vehicle's left flank. Amos fired a shot from one barrel, taking out the driver's side mirror, and forcing the plow to veer further right, toward the ice fishing village.

With only one headlight, a shattered windshield and no rearview mirror, Hank was driving nearly blind.

"Stick your head out and see where the hell we're going!" Jedidiah screamed.

"I don't want to get it blown off! That lunatic is right behind me!" Hank yelled back.

In the heat of the race, Amos felt the words of the prophet swell in his heart, and he exclaimed with full-throated zeal: *"For behold, the Lord commands, and the great house shall be struck down into fragments, and the little house into bits. Do horses run on rocks? Does one plow there with oxen? But you have turned justice into poison and the fruit of righteousness into wormwood!"*

Before the sermon had concluded, the first ice shack in the truck's path exploded upon impact with a splintering crash. Parts of the shanty, including its peaked roof, were launched into the air, while most of it was flattened beneath the charging plow. Ice augers, plastic buckets and other fishing gear went sailing. Hank and Jedidiah exchanged curses of surprise and

Snowplow Polka

blame. Before they could find a new course, another ice house had fallen victim to the rampaging truck, this one a good-sized aluminum box that had once been a tow-along camper. The flimsy siding crumpled, but the welded steel frame made the F-250 buck up and smack back down with a jarring slam. The truck's windshield collapsed in a shower of glass onto the robbers' laps. A bitter wind poured directly into the damaged cab, but now they could see.

"Turn left, Hank! Left! Get away from these shacks!"

Amos laughed out loud as the plow wreaked destruction on the ice houses of his tormentors. He dropped behind the skidding truck and urged the galloping Belgian into position along the passenger side, hoping the truck would circle back and take out even more shacks. The ice groaned and snapped in complaint, as new fissures spread ominously.

When Jedidiah saw the mounted rider come to his side of the truck, he poked his rifle out the window and tried to steady it.

Amos discharged the other barrel of his shotgun, peppering the rear panel with buckshot. "Take that, you heathens!"

Jedidiah quickly jerked his gun back in. Just as the truck clipped two more houses, the strained ice, already compromised by the holes drilled through it, cracked between the fishing holes like a dot-to-dot game.

As Amos pulled in the reins and brought Titus to a stop, he heard a voice in the cab scream, "Oh my God, we're goin' under!" The oversized truck, with no windows to form an air bubble, dove into the dark, icy void, the heavy plow blade leading the way.

"Do horses run on rocks?" exhaled Amos in amazement. The hermit watched, awestruck, as the vehicle disappeared—so quickly it was as if by magic. Only a glimpse of red taillights

Smite the Robbers

departing beneath the waves, a belch of icy water blowing upward from the open hole and then a ripple burbling over the rim of the new fissure betrayed the disaster site before all fell silent.

"Whoa, whoa, Titus. Attaboy," Amos soothed the agitated horse as he dismounted.

When he had seen the truck turn into the heart of the shantytown, he hadn't held out much hope for the snowplow's survival. With no intention of getting too close to the dark opening, he searched for ropes or plywood sheets that could be thrown out to any survivors. Still, he felt certain that no rescue efforts would be needed. The plow blade must have sent the unlucky truck to the bottom like an anchor. The only things moving on the dark water were lazily drifting bait buckets and chunks of floating ice.

Taking off his knit cap and holding it against his chest, Amos looked out upon the scene of destruction and spoke these somber words.

"I saw the Lord standing beside the altar, and he said: 'Smite the capitals until the thresholds shake, and shatter them on the heads of all the people; and those who are left of them I will kill with the sword; not one of them shall flee away; not one of them shall escape. The Lord God of hosts, he who touches the earth and it melts, and all who dwell in it mourn, and all of it rises like the Nile, and sinks again, like the Nile of Egypt; who builds his upper chambers in the heavens and founds his vault upon the earth; who calls for the waters of the sea and pours them out upon the surface of the earth—the Lord is his name."

❆

"Is everybody ready? We're almost there," said Rick Reinhart, prepping his family for arrival.

Snowplow Polka

"We're coming round the bend—I can see the Row Right Inn and Little Butternut ahead," added Vicky, following Rick's lead and turning to make sure the kids were looking, too.

"One, two, three . . . There's Grandma's house!"

"What's that flashing light on the lake?" Travis asked. "It looks like it's by Grandma's point."

"Wow, there's people and cars all over," Rick said. "Maybe there's been an accident on the ice."

After turning off the highway, everyone tried to recall exactly what they'd seen in the brief glimpse afforded them, which led to rampant speculation in the car. By the time Rick approached his mother's home, he had to stop short. The driveway was filled with vehicles, some of them police cars. He felt his body go rigid with fear as a uniformed officer came toward them with his hand raised and commanded, "Stop right there!"

"What's happening?" Rick murmured to Vicky. "That's a highway patrolman. What would he be doing here?"

The officer stopped beside the Subaru and bent down toward Rick's window. "I'm going to have to ask you to turn around and leave the premises, sir. This is a crime scene, not a tourist attraction."

In the opaque lenses of the highway patrolman's sunglasses Rick saw his own distraught reflection and his chin beginning to quiver.

"This is my mother's house," Rick said, choking up.

Vicky leaned over, coming to her husband's aid. "We just got here from the Cities. Can you tell us what's going on, Officer? Is Mrs. Reinhart alright?"

The policeman removed his aviator glasses, but his voice remained impersonal. "Stay in your car, folks. Do not get out of your vehicle. I'll let the designated authorities know you're here."

Smite the Robbers

"Designated authorities?" cried Rick. "Who are you? What about Ollie? Is he OK?"

"He won't answer you, Dad. He's not authorized." Travis seemed to understand police procedure and placed a hand on his father's shoulder. "I bet they're OK, Dad."

"Where's Grandma?" Tammy said in a shaking voice as she began to whimper.

The officer moved away, out of earshot. He tilted his head, spoke into a collar-mounted walkie-talkie and looked toward the crowd on the lake, trying to locate his colleague. Then he waited and kept an eye on the distraught family.

Luckily, the radio communication brought a quick response. The Reinharts saw a snowmobile coming off the ice toward them. The highway patrolman moved over to debrief the new arrival, but Helmuth walked right past him with barely a nod and then jogged to the car.

"Rick, Vicky, I'm glad you're here. We've been trying to reach you all morning."

"What's happened to my mom, Helmuth? Is she alright?"

"Can the two of you step out of the car so we can talk?" Helmut looked over at the children in the backseat. "I'm just going to talk to your mom and dad for a minute. Don't worry."

Vicky, Rick and the Sheriff moved a short distance away from the car. "The officer said this was a crime scene," Vicky told him. "What happened?"

"OK, we . . . we just don't know about your mom and Ollie yet. Their plow truck went through the ice out on the lake. It's just being dredged up now. But Amos claims the only people in the truck were two cabin robbers, and he's sure they're dead."

"Their truck went through the ice? Robbers were driving it?" Rick stammered, "Amos was there?"

"Rick, Vicky, I know this is hard on you," Sheriff Trost said,

Snowplow Polka

trying to soothe the couple. "Do you have a key to your mom's house? I want to look for evidence inside. Do you think you could call your uncle Richie and stay with them until we get a clearer picture of what's gone on here?"

"Evidence?" Rick's mind was reeling. "Yes, I've got a key. But we're not going anywhere till I find out what happened to my mother."

"You give the sheriff the key, dear," Vicky said. "I'll call your uncle and let him know we might have to come over."

Helmuth was someone they knew, and he contributed an honest sincerity to the conversation. Yet for all his supportiveness, he hadn't actually answered any of their questions. *It seems the authorities are just as clueless as we are*, Rick thought.

He handed over the house key. The sheriff took it and gently put his hand on Rick's arm. "I'm asking you to stay in your car. Let me do my job. We'll get to the bottom of this mystery. But before I go in, Rick, can you give me a brief layout of the house?" After Rick described the floor plan, Helmuth signaled to the highway patrolman. "Please stay with the family while I investigate the premises."

❄

Helmuth checked to make sure that the Reinharts were parked too far back to see him draw his gun and slip into the darkened front entryway.

In the foyer, he looked to his right and saw the stairs to the second floor bedrooms. Then, leading with his probing pistol, he turned left, slunk around the corner and entered the main room. A wide bank of floor-to-ceiling windows in the combined living/dining room gave a clear view out to the snow-drifted yard and beyond to the trees and lake.

Smite the Robbers

This airy space, bathed in morning sunlight, appeared perfectly undisturbed. *This doesn't look like a crime scene*, Helmuth thought. A red light from the telephone answering machine blinked incessantly on an end table as the sheriff proceeded through the living room, looking behind each piece of furniture. When he had gotten far enough into the dining area to see that the kitchen and back hallway were empty, he remembered: *Rick mentioned a home office.* Seeing a closed set of louvered doors across the living room, he approached, opened them and looked inside. *Oh . . . oh . . . something's wrong here.*

The desktop and floor were strewn with papers. He sniffed the air. *What stinks?*

Cautiously he entered the dimly lit office. *What a mess. It doesn't look vandalized though. It looks like Millie and Ollie just dropped everything and left in a hurry.*

The source of the smell was still a concern. *Hmm, what have we here? An open sardine tin and a lump of Limburger. I think I've found the culprit. Still, I'd better check behind the desk.* He shifted to his right, hoping he wouldn't see a dead body.

Just as he walked past a large bookcase, his peripheral vision registered an unexpected movement by the wall. Helmuth was already pressing the trigger when an object flicked toward him from the shadows.

The blast from the gun was deafening.

"Oh my God!" Helmuth yelled.

❄

Rick, Vicky, Travis and Tammy sat petrified in the car, their anxiety having risen to an unbearable level. At the sound of the gunshot, they all screamed. Rick peeked up and saw the highway patrolman leave them and rush toward the house.

Snowplow Polka

Rick could no longer contain himself, "Keep down everyone! I gotta see what happened!"

Despite his family's protests he got out of the car and stood as tall as possible to get a clearer view. A moment later, an object about the size of a shoebox was tossed out the door of his mom's house, landing in a snowbank. When both officers came out together, it looked safe enough for him to approach. The sheriff and patrolman saw him coming, but didn't caution him to stay away. They were looking at the object writhing in the snow.

All three men stared at the squirming victim. "Don't wor . . . be hap . . . be hap . . . ooh oo-ooh."

Big Mouth Billy Bass had taken a direct hit to the upper abdomen, just below his dorsal fin. The mechanical fish was still flipping, but its movement was now spastic—in brief, repetitious thumps. Still bound to its splintered plaque, the mortally wounded automation would begin to project its head, but then it would shudder back prematurely, all the while gasping out the same disjointed tune bits in a loop. "Don't wor . . . be hap . . . be hap . . . ooh oo-ooh."

Not knowing what else to do, the observers waited for the sad bass to expire. When it was obvious that its dirge would continue until the battery died, Helmuth unholstered his Glock and ended Big Mouth Billy's garbled last testament with a shot to the head.

"Thank you, Sheriff," Rick exhaled.

"Your parents weren't inside. I'm sorry I had to discharge a firearm in there, but I had to make a quick decision when that thing made its move. Aside from that, the house seemed completely empty and undisturbed. It did smell a little fishy, but I think your mom must have been eating sardines—there was an empty tin, and some cheese wasn't put away."

Smite the Robbers

Rick thought for a minute. Then said, "I know they were going to the Christmas polka dance last night. Were they there?"

"I did see your mom and Ollie at the dance, and they were fine," the sheriff said reassuringly. "I saw them again around three in the morning, too, at a party at your uncle Richie's cabin."

"Really? At three o'clock in the morning?" Rick looked amazed. "Did they leave the party then? What time did the accident with the truck happen on the lake?"

"I rousted all the partygoers out of your uncle's place and told them to go home. Amos said that the plow truck went through the ice at about four a.m. The neighbors around the lake agreed—that's when they heard gunfire."

"Gunfire?" Rick gasped.

A squad car with its siren blaring and lights flashing came into the driveway and redirected their attention. Two officers got out and came toward them. "We have some news, Sheriff," a policeman said after glancing at Rick.

"Give your report," Helmuth directed. "This is the son of one of the missing persons."

"OK. A Pontiac Bonneville was found parked behind the barn on the neighboring property."

"That would be Nels Gustafson's barn," Rick concluded.

"Was it a dark green four-door?" asked Helmuth. "We've had an APB out for that vehicle for about a week. We think it's the car the cabin robbers have been using. That places them at the scene of the crime."

"So you think these guys stole my mom's truck?" Rick was still trying to follow the chain of events. "Was Ollie driving the Buick last night? Is that car in the garage?"

"By God, I never got to the garage before that damn fish

Snowplow Polka

caught me off guard," the sheriff said. "I'll go back in, but Rick, you better stay with your family."

Rick did as he was told and headed back to the Subaru while Helmuth returned to the house.

Voices rang out all at once as Rick reached his family.

"What were those gunshots, Dad?"

"Honey, what did Helmuth discover?"

"Where's Grandma? What about Ollie?"

Rick tried to answer everyone. "The sheriff got scared by Big Mouth Billy Bass and accidently shot it. Those cops who just came said they found the robbers' car, but there's still no sign of Mom and Ollie."

"Dad, can we go into Grandma's house yet?" Travis pleaded.

No, Travis, we can't go in the house. It's a crime scene, and Helmuth is still checking things out."

"But Dad—Dad!" Travis leaned out from the car window and beckoned his father over. In a strained whisper he implored, "Can't I just go in the house to use the bathroom? I gotta go real bad!"

Rick understood his son's pained look. "You're gonna have to take a walk up the driveway till you're out of sight."

As Travis started toward the road, Rick heard the squeal of the garage doors opening. He turned around to see both stalls sitting empty.

❄

"Did you open a candy bar?" Millie asked. "I know you did, and it's a Snickers, too. A Three Musketeers smells more malty. I suppose that was the last one."

Smite the Robbers

"I thought you were out," Ollie replied. "I got so hungry it woke me up."

"Can you see the time?"

"I can't see a thing,"

They were in near darkness except for some faint blue light filtering through the cracked windshield. "I guess we were both knocked out. What happened?"

"We were run off the road by our own snowplow. Remember? Do you think that thief could still be around?"

"That had to be hours ago. I can see daylight now."

"Did you hear that? Sounded like a gunshot!"

"Wait, wait, I hear a siren—that's got to be the police. They must be looking for us. We gotta signal 'em!" Millie began to poke around on the dashboard. "What's working?"

"I can feel the keys in the ignition. I'll turn it to accessories. Let's see if the battery is dead."

"You honk the horn. I'll turn on the radio real loud and send up the antenna."

❄

Travis finally found a spot far enough away to avoid prying eyes. In the midst of his relief, a blaring honk came from the drift he was christening. Then the strains of the "Beer Barrel Polka" could be heard from under the snow. As Travis watched in disbelief, the shiny silver tip of an antenna poked through the frozen crust, telescoped out and then retracted, disappearing.

Travis ran back to the car with his arms flailing. "Mom! Dad! You guys gotta see this!"

Raise Your Cane

"We're looking for Mildred Reinhart and Oliver—"

"Room 404."

"You know them, and what room they're in?"

The cheery receptionist in the lobby smiled at the visiting family. "We don't get that many celebrities at Riceland General."

"You have them in the same room?" Rick asked, returning the humor. "They're not married, you know."

"They're in separate beds," the woman replied with a wink.

"Merry Christmas!" Tammy said as she plucked a candy cane from a red felt stocking she was carrying and put it on the receptionist's desk.

Snowplow Polka

❄

"Thanksgiving at the casino, and now Christmas at the hospital," Rick murmured under his breath to Vicky as the elevator doors closed.

"This will be a year to remember," Vicky replied from behind an armful of gifts. "The wonderful thing is, they're safe and we can still celebrate the holidays together."

Carrying a miniature decorated tree, Travis beamed proudly. "I think this is the coolest Christmas ever! I'm the one who saved them! I'm a hero!"

Tammy looked at her brother in admiration. "You're a superhero! Your picture is gonna be in the *Upper Mainz Rheinlander*!"

"Grandma! Ollie!" The kids charged into the hospital room and ran to their grandmother's open arms.

"Well at last! Some visitors I actually want to see. Give me a kiss right here, my Christmas elves," she said, pointing to her cheek.

Ollie grinned when he saw the gift basket Rick was carrying. "I hope some pistachios are in there!"

"How are you two feeling today? Vicky asked. "Still stiff? Has the doctor said anything else?"

"We're *still* perfectly fine—just a few bumps and bruises," Millie answered. "The doctor said I shouldn't be sleeping out all night in a car though, even if it is a Buick."

"They never should have brought us to a hospital. I don't know what for," Ollie added.

"They brought us here for observation, Ollie. Did you forget? We got knocked out!"

"My God, we were so afraid for you!" Vicky said. "Seeing you folks come out of that car was the greatest Christmas present ever. Travis, why don't you put the tree over there by the window with the gifts. Tammy, you arrange the cards."

"I'm sure gonna appreciate this holiday after a close call like we just had," Ollie declared as he looked around at the happy kids and all the gifts. "But it wasn't a very happy ending for those darn robbers. It looks like the truck is a goner, too."

"So, I guess that's the end of your snowplowing business?" Rick surmised, trying to sound disheartened.

"Yah, and it was going so good, too! The whole village said we were the best plowers they've had in years."

Rick attempted some consolation. "I gotta believe that a scare like this would make you want to sit back and just enjoy life more—relax and be thankful for your good health."

"You're right," Ollie affirmed. "I was thinking that for our next business I'd try to stay on the management side—let someone younger do the heavy lifting."

"Your . . . next business?"

"Sure. I'm cooking up a little something with Gustafson and a few of the other farmers in the area."

"Is it something you can tell us about?" Vicky asked, moving closer to Ollie's bed.

"We all made a vow not to tell anyone," Ollie said, leaning forward with an air of intrigue. "But this here plan should put food on the table and some money in our pocket, for sure."

"Are you a part of this business venture too, Mom?" Rick asked.

"Oh Ricky, now I hope you won't be critical. I know you weren't too happy about the snowplowing business, but you've gotta admit, we were a success—till the truck went into the lake."

"You're right. It sounds like you two were doing a good job."

Snowplow Polka

Millie turned toward Ollie and gave him a nod of her head, "I think we can share this good news with our family."

Ollie squirmed in his elevated bed and looked warily toward the open door of their room. Vicky took the hint and went over to close it. The whole family gathered around their beds. As much as he hated to unveil his secret, Ollie found the rapt attention exciting—plus, he figured some practice on his sales pitch couldn't hurt.

"Now, don't breathe a word of this outside the room, and don't pass judgment till you hear all the facts."

"I think I can handle that," Rick said. "So, what will your enterprise involve?"

"This time we won't be in the service industry, we're going to produce a product."

"Is it a craft product, something handmade?" Vicky asked with excitement.

Rick hesitated, and then, unable to bear the tension, asked, "So what's the product?"

"Jerusalem artichokes!" Ollie decreed.

Tammy wrinkled her nose. "Artichokes, ick!"

"The kind you eat?" Vicky asked.

"There really are some good ways to cook them," Millie stated with motherly pride. "I've got the cookbook *Jerusalem Artichokes for All Seasons*, and I'm dying to give some of those recipes a try."

"You can eat them, sure, but it's all about fuel," Ollie explained. "The tubers of this plant produce fructose, just like sugar beets. Their real value comes from making them into ethanol! Our country's energy independence could be a dream come true, thanks to this wonder plant."

Whether further facts were on their way or not, Rick couldn't contain himself. "But that was a huge Ponzi scheme in the '80s! Don't you remember how many farmers lost money in that disaster?"

Ollie scoffed. "Those hawkers in the '80s over-sold the concept. It's all different now."

"What's different? What's changed?" Rick sputtered.

Ollie was now prepared for his pitch. "I know you may have heard of some unfortunate people who lost money in the past, when swindlers with no good business sense tried to promote this product before its time. Today, scientists have narrowed the thirteen hundred varieties of that plant to the few that are really profitable. Back then, gas was less than a buck a gallon—now it's been almost four, and it'll go up. Back then, no cars or tractors were equipped to even burn ethanol—now it's a requirement. But the corn they're using is too expensive. And we need that corn for food, dagnabbit!"

With each point, Ollie stuck out another finger and ticked off the insurmountable evidence that would shame any doubter in his flock. He almost appeared to be levitating off his hospital bed as the conjoined threads of prosperity and patriotism took on quasi-evangelical overtones.

"But Ollie, you and Mom don't have any fields anymore," Vicky observed. "Who's going to grow them?"

"That's what I meant when I said Gustafson and some other farmers would work with us. They got the land, and I got the business sense, and we'll get some additional spare change from our insurance claims on the truck and car."

"And who would make the ethanol?" Rick challenged.

"That's the greatest part of all! But," the zealot whispered, "it has to stay top secret. The corn growers built way too may ethanol plants. There's one all ready to go and for sale, right now, near Clinton's Hollow. Gustafson and me toured it. All the pieces are falling into place. We'll be looking for investors."

Snowplow Polka

Millie leaned on one elbow and pointed to her son. "Rick, this could be a golden opportunity for you. You're one of the first to hear about it."

The door opened, and a perky nurse entered the room and trilled, "Hello everyone. Just a reminder: Your friend is performing now in the Great Hall over at the rehabilitation center. Family and friends are all invited to go to the dance."

"Reggie's here?" Vicky asked, looking relieved that Ollie's business proposition had been interrupted and Rick would have no time to reply to his mother's invitation.

Millie smiled. "Oh yah, he always visits the hospitals, ya know. But he made sure to come see us here today, alright."

"You kids go on ahead." Ollie dismissed the family with a flip of the wrist. "Your mom and I better put some clothes on, or the dance will get a bit too risqué for those old folks."

❄

"Let's watch the dance from the second-floor balcony," Rick suggested as they got back into the elevator. "There are some comfortable chairs in that lounge, and there's a vending machine for the kids to get a snack. I think I need to sit down."

Vicky put an arm around her husband. "Your Christmas gift wasn't what you expected?"

The sounds of happy laughter and a polka version of "Jingle Bells" mingled in the Great Hall. The Reinharts looked over the balcony railing at the merrymakers below.

Reggie was the unquestioned master of hospital and nursing home entertainment. He had dropped into a wheelchair and began performing "You Rock, I'll Roll."

Raise Your Cane

> You rock and I'll roll.
> You're gonna clap time to my wheelchair stroll,
> there in your rocking chair, beautiful soul.
> We'll be dancin' with the rhythm of love, love, love,
> till we're swingin' in the heaven's above.

Reggie had developed the ability to propel the chair with his elbows, leaving both hands free to play the accordion. Forward and backward the musician darted, planting a rubber-soled boot on the floor to brake quickly before spinning off in another direction with impressive agility. These antics made the patients squeal with feigned alarm. Reggie could even operate his tambourine leggings, and also an antique bicycle horn he had clipped to the chair right near his knee. He delighted the chair-bound residents by zooming at them with reckless speed, slamming on his brakes at the last second and honking the horn before jetting away.

"And here's another favorite!" Reggie called out.

> If you're happy and you know it, spin your wheels.
> If you're happy and you know it, walk your walker.
> If you're happy and you know it, then you really ought
>   to show it.
> If you're happy and you know it, raise your cane.

At this point, Rick and his family saw Millie and Ollie enter the hall. Reggie played a quick ascending charge on his keyboard to draw everyone's attention.

"Here they are!" the grandiose ringmaster proclaimed while applause broke out. "You may have heard about these two local heroes who saved the Upper Mainz Polka Club's Sunday Christmas dance. Then some bad guys knocked them

Snowplow Polka

into the ditch. But you can't keep these two seniors down. Millie, Ollie, take the floor."

As Reggie's accordion sprang back to life and the residents and their families formed a circle around the triumphant couple, Ollie bowed and then spun Millie in a dancing twirl.

Watching from above, Vicky snuggled against Rick and put her head on his shoulder. "Your Mom and Ollie are so lucky to have each other and all their good friends and this great community to support them. I hope we'll be just as happy and healthy and full of life when we get to their age, don't you, honey?"

Rick looked at the spinning activity below—a carousel of do-si-do-ing wheelchairs and slow-moving dancers. His mother and her beau were at the center of it all—loved and loving it, happy and spreading happiness, old but living it.

If you're happy and you know it, raise your cane.

Ambrose McGuine (rhymes with "wine")
is in fact David and Valerie Atkinson, a husband
and wife writing team. Both graduated
from the Minneapolis College of Art and Design
and worked in the St. Paul Public Schools.

Snowplow Polka was inspired by the many
colorful characters and welcoming locales
they have encountered in northwest Wisconsin
on umpteen trips to visit relatives and friends.

They are now retired and reside in the Twin Cities,
where they find the snow plowing services
to be, for the most part, acceptable.

Acknowledgments

We would like to thank our executive editor,
Ann Delgehausen, of Trio Bookworks, who saw potential
in the manuscript we considered to be "done." She sensed
what we were capable of, and her encouragement and
guidance allowed us to bring *Snowplow Polka* to its finished
form. Thanks also go to our developmental editor,
Kellie Hultgren, of KMH Editing, for her help in molding
a collection of quirky vignettes into a coherent story.

Special thanks to Kevin Cannon, who captured
the humor of the story in his comic renditions
for the cover and interior art.

Also, we thank Pete Rechtzigel for musical advice
and for introducing us to his father's composition
"How Do You Know There Ain't No Beer In Heaven?"